The Female Disciplinary Manual

Authorised for use in Schools, Universities, Colleges and other institutions undertaking the teaching or training of young ladies.

Also recommended for use in the private household and in places of employment.

Also Published
by The Wildfire Club

THE CORPORAL PUNISHMENT OF SCHOOLGIRLS
A documentary survey by Miss Margaret Stone

THE FEMININE RÉGIME
The acclaimed novel by Miss Regina Snow

HAPPY TEARS
A 1930s disciplinary classic

The Female Disciplinary Manual

A Complete Encyclopædia of the Correction of the Fair Sex

Produced by the Standing Committee on Female Education

WILDFIRE

A Wildfire Club Edition

Set in Monotype Bembo
at the Imperial Press

First Clothbound Edition
Fourth Impression
3,500 copies of this edition in print

Printed and bound in Great Britain by Antony Rowe Ltd., Chippenham, Wiltshire
on 21-lb Felsted Cream Wove : Demy Octavo (8¾" x 5½")

CONTENTS

Part 2: Corporal Punishment

Introduction

Availability, pricing & conditions of display of this book Objectives & Definitions — Discipline & Educational Theory — The Formation of Character — The New Sensibility — Correct Levels of Discipline.

THIS TREATISE HAS been issued by the Imperial Department of Education to give practical and theoretical instruction in the various methods and procedures for the discipline of girls and young women. In accordance with Section 52, Paragraph I (B) of the Education Act of 2032, at least three copies must be retained by all girls' and mixed schools, women's University colleges, colleges of education, secretarial colleges, teaching hospitals, corrective establishments and all other institutions, public and private, concerned with the education or training, full-time or part-time, of females under the age of twenty-one years. One copy shall be retained by the Head Mistress or Principal of the institution; one shall be kept in the Staff Room, Senior Common Room or equivalent meeting-place where it must be available for consultation by any member of staff at any time; and the third shall be kept in the library or other main place of reference where it shall be retained by the librarian as a work of reference. It shall be issued upon request to any member of the teaching staff to be consulted in the library or place of reference but not to be removed therefrom. Further copies may be obtained from the Imperial Stationery Office or from main Post Offices at nineteen shillings and sixpence (plus 6d postage if ordered by post). It is recommended that all female members of the staff of establishments which may be concerned at any time with the discipline of female pupils, scholars or employees should possess a copy of this manual, and the governing bodies of such establishments are encouraged to issue it to all such members. For this purpose it is made available in pamphlet form at the rate of 2s.6d. each for orders of more than six copies and 2s. each for orders of more than twelve copies. It is available to members of the general public at the standard price of 3s. 6d. and is recommended in particular to the attention of mothers and mistresses of domestic maidservants.

Principal Objectives & Definitions

THE SCOPE OF the work is limited to the correction of female miscreants by female disciplinarians: and although much of what appears herein may be applied to the disciplining of both sexes, the differences are sufficient to make it desirable to issue a treatise specifically designated for the use of feminine institutions. That there is a difference between the masculine temperament and the feminine, in these matters as in most others, is today no longer disputed, and one wonders with some incredulity how it ever could have been, although we are assured that a few short decades ago, in the later 20th century, it was disputed, and indeed more or less "officially" denied. One can only marvel at the strange *naïveté* and self-deception of those bygone days. In many passages we have dealt with discipline in the light of the New Sensibility, and it is our belief that girls and women, on the whole, have a more heightened attunement to the subtle currents which may be set in motion by the exercise of discipline.

Of course some members of the stronger sex have the highest refinement of spirit. Men have played an important rôle in the development of the New Sensibility, but it is our belief that the average feminine sensibility is considerably in advance of the average masculine sensibility, especially in later childhood. The intense and pure current with which some sections of our more disciplined girls' schools may become charged seems to us a less probable phenomenon in an equivalent masculine establishment, and one which, if it did arise, might be in greater danger of developing in an unhealthy (and unsubtle) direction.

Discipline is a matter of especial importance to the feminine portion of the population. In the home, the duty of discipline falls most often and most naturally upon the mother. Domestic maidservants are once again widely employed, and their care and discipline falls almost always upon the mistress of the house. Many more children than hitherto are now educated at home—almost always by a governess—and the teaching profession, except in boys' private schools, is predominantly feminine. Indeed, the present writer would venture the opinion that there is a case for saying that even boys' schools might benefit from having a mistress in charge of the administration of more serious punishments, and this for three reasons: 1) that punishment should have a protective or maternal aspect, and the maternal instinct is, as demonstrated by scientific research, much stronger than the paternal, 2) that punishments administered by women are less prone to have an undertone of violence or competitiveness, 3) that the sensibility which we consider to be more marked, upon average, in women can make of discipline an enriching, refining and improving experience.

We wish to add that these remarks, in common with others which treat of the sensibility of discipline, do not represent the views or policy of Her Imperial Majesty's Government, but are those of the authors of this manual. In this treatise we have in mind, before all else, the position of a mistress in a girls' school; however most of what we say is easily applicable to the governess in charge of girls, and, to a slightly lesser extent, mothers, mistresses in charge of maidservants, housekeepers, office supervisors and other institutional directresses. In many cases it is our belief that methods of discipline which traditionally have been largely restricted to the scholastic sphere may be beneficially applied outside the world of the school. This is already becoming accepted in some measure with the introduction of the cane into ladies' colleges, teaching hospitals and other institutions, and it is our belief that it should be, and will be, more widely applied and applied in a greater variety of ways in the stricter, smarter, more sensitive world of today.

Discipline and Educational Theory

THIS IS HARDLY the place to go deeply into the realms of modern educational theory, but it would seem apposite to put forward one or two remarks. The years after the collapse of the European Federation have seen a revolution in educational theory as the hidebound 20th-century ideas which had been so rigorously maintained by the European bureaucracy could at last be freely called into question.

Of course, these ideas had already ceased to have much intellectual force for some years, but the educational world was compelled by a labyrinthine system of regulations and State-patronage to continue to pay lip-service to them. With the demise of this unwieldy and retrograde bureaucracy, new ideas came rapidly to the fore, and the writings of Mr. C.V. Carleton, Professor Mirandella and Dr. Maria Weiss formed the basis for a complete overhaul of educational theory.

We shall not concern ourselves with a summary of the new theories of education except insofar as they concern the subject of discipline. Essentially the old theory of education was "child-centred". It held that children should not be compelled to study, but should be taught by holding their interest. This went hand in hand with the provision of a vast range of "entertainments", always trivial and unintelligent and usually unwholesome, through the channels of television, "pop" music (a very different thing from the popular music of our own day) *&cetera*. The result of all this was that children developed what, in the rather pompous jargon of the time, was called a steadily decreasing "attention span", which, being interpreted, means that they were unable to concentrate upon any one thing for more than a few minutes at a time, and only then if the object of concentration was tricked out for their delectation with gaudy and distracting "gimmicks" of some sort.

Unsurprisingly, educational standards dropped rapidly. A first year undergraduate in 1999 was generally incapable of doing work intended for sixteen-year-old school pupils in 1959. In the sciences, the first year at university was spent in attempting to provide undergraduates with the grounding in mathematics they had formerly brought with them from school. Adult literacy declined alarmingly throughout the last third of the 20th century, and many other indices of decline might be cited.

Once again, on looking back at the tenacity with which the educational theorists of the time clung to the belief that their egalitarian and pseudo-libertarian nostrums represented an "advance" over earlier ideas which, in every measurable respect, had produced vastly superior results—whether one looks at the standards of the Universities or at the literacy of the humblest school-leaver—one can only marvel at the *naïveté* and self-deception of those strange and deluded decades. It was only natural that the new educational theorists should re-assert the principle that a school should be a place of discipline, and that its function was to train the minds of children rather than to let them grow wild. Obviously it must teach them to concentrate for progressively longer periods upon the task before them whether or not they found it immediately congenial. The mind must be stretched, not left to its natural flabbiness. Smartness and order must be encouraged in every sphere, from uniform to the setting out of a written page, and entertainments must be of a sort which promote healthy development rather than anarchic self-indulgence.

In his seminal book *Education for the Free**, Mr. Carleton pointed out that a disciplined education was one which produced independent, firm, resolute minds, while an education in which the child was constantly "enticed" with gimcrack gewgaws produced a will-less, mental serf, an ideal passive "consumer", superficially rebellious and cynical but fundamentally the malleable plaything of whoever controlled the centralised machinery of "entertainment" and "information". No doubt this is why the old theories were maintained for so long by bureaucracies such as that of the European Federation, and why, from its earliest inception, the European bureaucracy was implacably hostile to the discipline of children (as were the tame "intellectuals" of the period who always, wittingly or unwittingly, promoted the aims of entrenched power), forcing, for example, the abolition of corporal punishment in State schools of this country long before the Federation was even in existence.

With the end of "Europe", discipline returned to education: drilling and rote-learning were an ideal corrective for damaged "attention spans"; intellectual rigour and higher standards of study raised performance and attainment at every level. Smart, crisply-uniformed children replaced the plastic-clad circus-clowns of the previous generation. Then came the famous Hampstead School case in which a mother sued the school for serious injury caused to her child through a fall from a roof occasioned by bullying. The judge severely admonished the headmistress for continuing to run her school without corporal punishment and thus allowing con-

* Published by Hall & Noble at 17s 6d.

ditions of disorder and indiscipline in which such things could happen. For many schoolmistresses, this was the point when it became clear that not only was the administration of corporal punishment no longer somewhat frowned upon, but that failing to administer it when it was needed could be an occasion for the gravest censure. Corporal punishment, in short, is not simply a right possessed by schoolmistresses: it is a solemn duty.

The Formation of Character

THE VALUE OF discipline in forming the character of children is a matter to which modern educational theorists have paid considerable attention. For a period of several decades, beginning in the 1960s, the assertion that discipline had a part to play in forming the character was uniformly received by the petty-intelligentsia of the time with a mockery so predictable and stereotyped that it might have been rehearsed (it was not, of course, rehearsed, merely conditioned). This mockery would appear to have been based upon nothing other than ignorant prejudice, and two or three generations of un-formed and increasingly de-formed characters have convinced most people that there is something in the notion of character-forming after all.

It is, of course, not in the more limited sense of punishment alone that discipline forms the character. In demanding a smartness of appearance, it fosters self-respect and a degree of self-confidence. The child is taught to perceive herself as an upright and attractive representative of her school, her nation and of the dignity of humanity, rather than a sloppy, casual creature which, for all its bellicose "assertiveness" is incapable of winning respect from any one, itself included. In teaching the child to apply herself to tasks which she may find uncongenial, discipline fosters the habit of self-command. It teaches her to subordinate her fleeting impulses to her decided aims, and thus renders her more effective in achieving whatever she wishes to achieve; making her a capable, independent person rather than a plaything of her transient passions and of whoever has the means of manipulating those passions.

At the same time, discipline teaches obedience; it helps the individual to act as part of a greater unit without losing her individuality; it fosters a coöperative team spirit rather than a selfish egotism. Only she who has learned to obey can learn to command, and the woman who can command the respect, love, loyalty and obedience of her children and her servants must first have been schooled herself in the acceptance of discipline. The old commercial-bureaucratic world-order, which culminated with the European Federation, did not want a world bound together with bonds of love, loyalty, respect and obedience. It wanted a world of atomised, proletarianised, isolated individuals, unable to coöperate or trust one another and thus wholly ineffective and utterly dependent upon "Big Brother".

To this end it fostered everywhere a cult of false independence, character-destroying self-indulgence and complete indiscipline. It waged unremitting war upon domestic service, parental authority, human decency, self-respect and every other element of social health and cohesion, finding a perfect vehicle for the promotion of its policies in the sequacious "intellectuals" of the time. The result, unsurprisingly, was not only social tyranny but individual misery, with suicide, crime, divorce, mental illness and every other index of despair rising to unprecedented levels. In the last quarter of the 20th century one in four adults sought help for mental disorder—a truly astonishing figure, and psychiatrists reported that the underlying problem in most cases was (to use once again, at the risk of bringing a smile to the faces of our readers, the overblown jargon of the times): "lack of life-content"—in other words, the hollowness both of a society unrelievedly trivial, ugly and sub-standard and of individuals whose flabby, undisciplined, un-formed characters left them bereft of interior resources and of the capacity for taking a real interest in life.

Conversely, the child educated according to the modern theory has been trained to apply her mind to objects of interest. Rather than waiting passively to be "interested" or "stimulated" by something—a task which becomes less and less possible as the palate becomes increasingly inured to ever more sensational, vulgar and easily-assimilated stimuli—the modern girl has been trained to apply herself, to exercise disciplined *active appreciation* which enables her to find the deepest and most absorbing interest in literature and art, to appreciate the æsthetics of modern design and the fine points of whatever she may turn her mind, her eye or her ear to. Rather than being bombarded with garish and worthless "stimuli" she has been brought up in an atmosphere of purity and discipline which has honed her sensibility and sharpened her powers of appreciation.

This refined æsthetic sense, the heightened appreciation of the fine shades of things, which has been termed the New Sensibility of our times is, we would argue, in no small degree related to the return of discipline. No one can deny that we have in this generation an extraordinary efflorescence of literary and artistic activity; a remarkable increase in the appreciation of the arts; an intellectual and artistic vigour among the higher orders of society and an increasing delicacy and fineness among the lower orders which may reasonably be termed a spiritual renaissance—and one in which this country is noticeably in advance of most of the countries of Europe which have held on for longer to the old outlook. To say that the New Sensibility is the product of greater discipline in schools and elsewhere would be both a foolish exaggeration and an oversimplification; there are many other factors at work, and in any case, not only has discipline fostered the New Sensibility, but the New Sensibility has also fostered a new understanding and appreciation of discipline. It is this phenomenon which we propose briefly to consider now.

Discipline and the New Sensibility

THE EXPRESSION "the New Sensibility", which is so widely used nowadays, is one which (like many other important concepts) defies precise definition. It refers to the newly-awakened sense of beauty, the new appreciation of fine shades, the subtler and purer awareness of things, which has flowered with the demise of the cheap, sloganised, pre-packaged mass-culture of the late 20th century and the earlier years of this.

Some would consider the New Sensibility to be the sensibility of an æsthetic minority, yet it is hard to deny that the sensibility of every level of society has been refined and purified to an extent which would have seemed hardly credible a generation ago. There is a romanticism abroad and a new innocence: an almost complete absence of the jaded cynicism of the old régime. In its most concentrated form, the New Sensibility may belong to the velvet-clad Bohemian circles of Oxford and Pimlico, but there is scarcely a schoolgirl who has not read Vemera Lynton or seen *The*

Silver Dream and is not affected to some extent by the new Romanticism. The very popular music she hums on her way to school—songs like "Evangeline" and "Moonlight Memories"—are shot through with a sensibility which none can deny is delicate and fine, and, if compared to the popular "music" of a few decades ago, would seem positively ætherial.

As we have indicated, there seems little doubt that discipline has played its part in helping to create this higher state of sensibility. It is important also to understand that this sensibility has played a considerable part in the application of discipline, especially in female establishments. In discussing, for example, the imposition of various punishments, we shall be discussing not only legalistic questions of severity, but subtle questions concerning the *tone* and *colouring* of a punishment and its variant forms. This may seem rather esoteric, but girls respond to it very well, and when a sensibility of discipline is developed by sensitive mistresses within a school of girls of above-average intelligence, the result can be at once a marked refinement of general sensibility and a considerable raising of standards, both academic and of every other sort.

We shall speak occasionally of disciplinary *rapports*. Such a *rapport* may be formed between a mistress and a whole class, producing an intense and highly creative atmosphere. Deeper *rapports* may be formed between individuals. They are sometimes formed between a mistress and a girl, though this is limited by the mistress's time and the fact that she must give full attention to all her pupils. Often they occur between a prefect and a younger girl, the prefect giving considerable disciplinary attention to her *protégée* (usually a sensitive and intelligent younger girl) and often leading her into a deeper sensibility.

The attitude of mistresses to this has been, on the whole, far more enlightened than it would have been a generation ago. The value of such intense and sometimes severe friendships has been generously recognised, and while they have not been actively promoted, they have not been interfered with unless there has been some other cause for concern. This approach is, in our view, that which should be adopted by the mistress toward these youthful *rapports*. Without prying, she should keep a discreet eye open to ensure two things: the first is that the younger girl is actually *en rapport* with her mentor, without which such attentions may be unduly distressing to the child and may seem like a form of bullying.

Of course one should not stop a prefect from "taking a girl in hand" against her will where necessary, nor will a genuine *rapport* be without its moments of bitter-sweet distress. A mistress must keep a very sensitive finger on the pulse of the situation. Where *rapports* of this type become the "rage" in a school, it is sometimes judicious to allow younger girls to appeal against prefects' punishments. Of course, such appeals will be summarily dismissed, usually with extra punishment, unless the prefect's discipline (or its frequency) is genuinely excessive or unmerited. This will make such appeals a rarity, but it does have the effect of giving any girl the ability to escape from a disciplinary *rapport* which is distressing to her, the more so since true *protégées* regard the attentions of their mentors as a privilege and would not dream of appealing against them, however severe they might be; while the girl who does appeal will be immediately dropped by her mentor as unworthy of her attentions. Only a girl who wants to be dropped will appeal, but she should have the chance of doing so. In schools where this system has been adopted, mistresses have usually been mildly surprised by how rare an appeal is, and how mutual most *rapports* appear to be. In one case the system was introduced with the precise intention of allowing a particular girl—who was known to be writing numerous long and apparently gratuitous impositions for a particular prefect—to appeal: however she did not, and when asked specifically if she would like to appeal, reacted with something akin to thinly veiled disdain.

The second thing a mistress must look for is any suggestion of improper *liaison*. This, however (whatever may be the case with boys, and whatever may have been the case with girls in the days when all children were subjected to a massive propaganda assault on their innocence), is a very rare thing among girls. This last point leads us, perhaps, into the heart of the New Sensibility as it affects this area of discipline.

In the old days, the Freudian view of human nature led most people to assume that any rapport of this sort must have unsavoury connotations. This Freudian view was part of the overall reductionism of the old "modernist" outlook. All things must be reduced to their coarsest and basest possibilities. Chartres

Cathedral was a mere by-product of economics; the most rarefied and subtle of human passionate attachments are nothing more than deviations of the animal procreative instinct. Any one who should discuss such attachments in terms of their unique and indefinable qualities rather than as mere variants of the procreative urge was dismissed as "pre-Freudian" or "*naïve*".

It is a cardinal point of the New Sensibility that this blunt-witted, undiscriminating reductionism has been discarded in favour of a renewed openness to the numberless colours and savours of life, a vigorous delicacy of appreciation which has unlocked the door to a new world of sensibility. It is something like a rebirth, or a transition from a two-dimensional world to a three-dimensional one; from a monochrome world to a world tinted with every hue and every combination of hues that the rainbow has to afford.

To achieve this new sensibility, one must be disciplined in the sense that one must be ready to put effort into the appreciation of life rather than imbibing it passively; and one must live in a world of purity and grace rather than one supersaturated with cheap and sub-standard stimulants. The discipline of a good school provides girls with the bases for such a sensibility, and in turn this sensibility can transmute that discipline into a higher and subtler thing than it has been before, and one which, in its turn, can raise girls to a yet higher level of sensibility.

A Correct Level of Discipline

OCCASIONALLY THE criticism has been levelled against the new educational system in some girls' schools that the discipline is too severe. This is not merely a criticism made by the diehard minority of social atavists who wish to return to the fœtid miasma of the late 20th century; it has also been raised by serious people who, while accepting the importance of neatness, discipline and high standards feel that in some cases they are pursued too rigorously and with too great an emphasis on punishment.

In most cases we think that such criticisms are the result of a misunderstanding. The cases where such severity is in force are almost always cases where a *rapport* of the type we have been discussing is in question. This, as we have already indicated, may take the form of an individual *rapport* between a senior and a junior girl or between a (usually senior) girl and a mistress, but it can also take place between a mistress and a whole class, and a level of discipline which would be, not excessive, but certainly rigorous under less heightened conditions can in fact be elevating, creative and quite happily accepted by the class, who usually not only achieve the highest standards, but have a greatly enhanced level of sensibility and creative achievement in and out of lessons. Under more "normal" circumstances, when such *rapports* do not exist (they tend to come about "naturally"—some mistresses are adept at forming them, but even for them some classes seem too pedestrian to make it possible), discipline, while firm, is usually an established thing which relies only occasionally upon punishment.

Of course this will vary. Some mistresses are always stricter than others. Some individuals and some classes require much more discipline than others, but we wish to correct the impression which a book like this might give that modern school life is a doleful round of lines, order marks, strappings and detentions enlivened only by the occasional caning. Obviously when such things are gathered together in one small volume, the overall effect may be a little oppressive; but the atmosphere of a modern school, while contained and strict, is on the whole a much happier one than that of the sloppy "lout-farms" of the previous generation: and the neat, attractively turned-out girl of today, her mind finely honed, her capacities stretched to the full, her perceptions active, her appreciation of a hundred different things generous and enthusiastic, her heart three years more innocent and her intellect three years more advanced, is far happier, far more charming, far more alive than her canvas-shod, soul-impoverished predecessor. This, and this alone, is the point, the purpose, the meaning of modern discipline.

Part One

NON-CORPORAL PUNISHMENT

PUNISHMENTS DIVIDE clearly into two major types—corporal and non-corporal. Corporal punishments are, and always have been, the most frequently administered in the home (despite a short-lived attempt to suppress them by legal—but nonetheless morally illegitimate—coercion at the beginning of this century), largely, one suspects, because most homes lack the atmosphere of formal authority to impose non-corporal punishments. We make no judgement as to which sort of punishment is best for the home (each type has its proper place), but we think it a good sign when a mother or aunt has the confidence and authoritativeness to set lines or impose some similar discipline when she considers it desirable.

We are pleased to observe that this sort of maternal authority is very much on the increase these days, and can only applaud it as a sign of moral and cultural health, though we doubt whether impositions, or even the increasingly popular household cane will ever displace, or even make significant inroads upon, the predominance of the impromptu maternal spanking. No doubt this is as it should be. In girls' schools, on the other hand (the case is often different in boys' schools), despite the widespread acceptance of the need for corporal punishment, non-corporal punishments are the general rule. There are honourable exceptions to this, and the position is slowly changing, but on the whole detentions and lines (in that order) are the commonest forms of chastisement, with the strap and the cane used rather more rarely. As we have said, that is not always so, and in many of the more advanced schools the strap, in particular, has come to the fore as a means of classroom discipline with the cane unseen but ever in the background as a final sanction, while in others the classroom cane has become a familiar aspect of school life.

The reasons for this partial aversion from corporal discipline in girls' schools has more than one cause. In some cases (particularly among older mistresses) there may be a residual lingering of the old-fashioned attitudes which believed that all physical discipline was in some way a Bad Thing (we are ashamed to say that attitudes of this type were more pronounced in the teaching profession than in many other walks of life). However, we have found this to be a very minor factor. More common is a strong and healthy reaction against the outmoded fetich of treating girls and boys as if they were identical. A number of mistresses consider corporal chastisement a "boys' thing" which should not be inflicted upon members of the more delicate sex. This is a much more serious objection and one to which we shall present our reply in a moment. There is also the fact that many older mistresses are simply unused to the practice of physical punishment and find it awkward, while mistresses as a whole lack the aggressive impulses which may sometimes make corporal punishment immediately appealing to schoolmasters.

Now, we would suggest that it is precisely this lack of aggressiveness which makes women better disciplinarians than men. A corporal punishment administered by a woman is never (or almost never) an attack. It is something far subtler, far deeper, and which has its ultimate root in the maternal function of nourishment. Of course, we are not suggesting that a responsible schoolmaster is attacking his pupils in disciplining them, but we are suggesting that the ultimate natures of masculine discipline and feminine discipline are radically different. We are inclined to think that boys in general would benefit from feminine discipline, but that is a matter far removed from the subject of this treatise. What we are sure of is that girls, upon the whole, respond to discipline in a different way from most boys, that it is a profounder, subtler experience which can enrich them and add a new dimension to their sensibility; one which will deepen their appreciation of many things that are quite unconnected with discipline—except that, in its broader sense, we should say that no aspect of human life is unconnected with discipline.

We are not suggesting that physical chastisement is the only means of producing this effect—indeed, the profoundest effects are sometimes produced by non-physical discipline—but we do suggest that it is often important in helping to produce it, and that, in its many forms, it contains myriad *nuances* which are wholly lost if it is excluded altogether. Most importantly, in answer to those who say that physical discipline is a masculine thing and that its imposition upon girls is a retrogressive act harking back to the purblind and dogmatic equalitarianism of the 20th century, we say that physical chastisement, practised by the fair sex upon the fair sex in a feminine setting, is a thing quite different from the masculine punishment which it may superficially resemble; a thing wholly feminine; a thing which should not be lost to the world, but which, on the contrary, in this age of subtle sensibility, should be understood and appreciated more fully, perhaps, than it has been these many centuries.

On a more mundane note, we should also say that there are certain practical advantages to the use of physical chastisement: not the least of which is that it takes up very little of a girl's time. Of course there are occasions—many occasions—when it may be considered entirely desirable that she should repent at tedious leisure for her transgressions over a lengthy imposition; but it is not always a good thing. Sometimes it is better to have the thing cleared up and forgiven in a brief, intense moment of purification.

We are by no means opponents of non-physical means of correction. Indeed, it will be seen that we have the highest regard for these punishments. In the ladies' University colleges, where the cane was introduced some time ago for serious breaches of college discipline, it was, and still often is, considered that this is the only form of discipline acceptable to a young lady over, or not much under, the age of twenty-one. Other punishments, it is often held, are too childish or humiliating. The introduction at Lady Margaret Hall of a College Detention on Saturday afternoon and even of a rudimentary prefectorial system in which lines are sometimes given has been considered whimsical by some and inappropriate by others. In our view it is entirely in keeping with the ladies' college which has been most associated with the development of the New Sensibility; and the formation of informal disciplinary circles at other ladies' colleges holding their own private detentions and awarding and accepting other penalties may seem mystifying to many, but is, we feel, a sign of the times and an indication of the lightness, delicacy and gentle grace of feminine discipline. It is also an indication that just as the exclusion of physical chastisement is deleterious to sensibility, so such chastisement on its own is insufficient, and young ladies may actually crave the slower, more tedious, yet subtly more enclosing forms.

1. Detention

Definition — Impromptu detentions & the uses of uncertainty — Formal detentions — Specific types of detention — Nature of detentions & ancillary tasks Fixed or indefinite periods — Combinations of detention types — Detention homework — Flexibility & variations The underlying psychology of detention — Its elegance as a punishment.

IN MANY GIRLS' schools today—perhaps in a majority of them—detention is the primary means of punishment. Where Order Marks★ are given, these are often "redeemable" in the form of detention. Lines†, the other most favoured of girls' school punishments, constitute the most usual imposition set during detentions, so that between them these two forms of correction hold a position of dominance in the disciplinary systems of our feminine educational establishments.

For obvious reasons this form of punishment is not much found outside schools, although some governesses employ it and detentions, while not a formal part of the discipline of ladies' University colleges have, in a few cases, been instituted by private disciplinary societies organised and voluntarily participated in by the young ladies themselves. Detention can take many forms and may vary in severity from the very mildest of punishments to one of the more severe.

At the lowest end of the scale we have the simple act of "keeping children in" for a short time after lessons. Usually a number of girls who have been badly behaved or inattentive during class will be told to remain behind when the other girls are leaving. Their detention may be as short as ten minutes during

★ See page 52 *et seq.*   † See page 31 *et seq.*

which time they may be set a short piece of copying or told to sit in silence, perhaps with their hands on their heads (particularly appropriate where their offence has been talking or restlessness in class), or, in some cases, the mistress, having told them to remain behind, may then ignore them, perhaps getting on with some marking or other work for ten minutes or so. The girls, so boisterous before, one may be sure will be quite silent in the almost-empty classroom, wondering what will happen to them and when they will be allowed to leave. After a suitable interval the mistress will address them with some well-chosen words of admonition and dismiss them.

Such punishment is greatly enhanced if girls are sometimes kept behind in a similar manner to receive the strap or impositions, or if such detentions are known sometimes to be much longer: this lends an aura of dreadful uncertainty to the period of waiting. Impromptu detentions of this sort may, as we have indicated, be rather longer in duration and may, indeed, be of no fixed duration: a common practice is to set some imposition such as a hundred lines or a piece of copying and instruct girls to raise their hands when they finish. This lends a certain *piquance* to the work, for girls are anxious to finish it quickly in order to release themselves from the detention. However, if the work does not meet the mistress's standards, all or part of it may be rejected and the girl who thought she was to leave first may be labouring over her repeated exercise as her classmates one by one present their finished impositions and gain their freedom. In some cases a girl presenting unsatisfactory work in her hurry to leave detention may find herself with her imposition doubled, and perhaps having to report back after lessons the next day—possibly sitting among detained girls from an older or a younger class of girls she does not know, re-doing the detention work of the previous day. Some mistresses, indeed, collect girls from different classes throughout the day for a detention at the end of it. Each girl is told to report to a particular room (usually the mistress's last classroom of the day) at the end of lessons where suitable punitive work is set for a stated or unstated period, or until it is satisfactorily finished. The girls in the last lesson who have been told to remain behind may be surprised to see a number of unknown girls arriving, causing them suddenly to realise that they have found themselves in a "real" detention. Detentions of this sort, which some mistresses hold at whim on a particular day, when they are perhaps tired of giving other punishments, can be said to stand midway between the impromptu detention discussed earlier and the formal detention.

The formal detention is the most usual kind, and most schools have a number of regular formal detentions during the week, usually with distinctive names. Not all of these will necessarily take place on any given week, as they may not always have "customers", but they are on the weekly agenda and any mistress (and in some cases prefects too) may enter a girl for any one of them. The variety of such detentions with their different names and characters is far too great for us to enter into here, many of them, indeed, being unique to a particular school, but let us give a few examples of the range of detentions that might be found in a school.

1) Prefects' Detention: duration half an hour. This detention is held from four o'clock to half-past four every day (lessons ending at ten to four) and is supervised by a prefect. Normally lines are given and a girl may be required to repeat the work in her spare time or to report for Prefects' Detention again the next day if her work is deemed unsatisfactory by the prefect in charge. This is the lightest, and, as it were, the "standard" detention. Girls are put down for it as a discipline for everyday infractions and some girls are fairly regular attenders. To appear too often at Prefects' Detention merits some more serious chastisement.

2) House Detention: duration normally between one hour and one hour and a half. This detention is held on Mondays and Thursdays and supervised usually by a senior prefect or a junior mistress. This is a rather more serious detention and the strap is given for the smallest fault (dropping a pencil, placing a ruler crookedly on the desk *&cetera*). Unsatisfactory work is repeated in girls' own time.

3) Evening Detention is held on Wednesdays. It begins at six o'clock and ends at the mistress's discretion, but rarely much before bedtime. Sometimes some girls are allowed to go earlier than others depending on their original offence and their behaviour in detention. A good strapping—not less than twelve strokes of the Middle-School Strap—is a part of this detention. Girls are called out at intervals during the detention to receive their punishment.

Extra strappings are, of course, given for every fault and many mistresses give "detention homework"—i.e. further lines to be done in the next few days. These, of course, are in addition to any repeated work which may be necessary.

4) Long Detention is held on Saturday afternoon, beginning at one o'clock and ending not earlier than five. Some girls may not be released at five and may have to stay on into the evening missing tea. A prefect or second mistress may be brought in to supervise this second part of the detention. Day girls, who are usually at home on Saturdays, must report in full uniform for Long Detention. Three statutory strappings of not less than twelve strokes each are given during this detention—usually one near the beginning, another before leaving and the third somewhere in the middle. The exception to this rule is when a girl is caned during Long Detention, which sometimes happens.

These, as we have said, are merely examples of the various kinds of regular formal detentions which may be held. *Ad hoc* formal detentions may be arranged for particular offences, and greater flexibility is afforded by the ability to combine detentions: "You will attend Prefects' Detention every day this week", for example, is a useful alternative to one of the longer detentions. We have known schools to have no fewer than a dozen different regular formal detentions. By no means all of them are held each week, of course, but each one has its own special character and is useful for particular purposes.

The Nature of Detentions

WE MUST NOW consider the nature of detentions—what form should they take? Should they be for fixed periods? What sort of imposition should be set? Of course there is no single answer to these questions, and it is important to consider the various merits of different approaches. As with other punishments, we shall find that different methods have a different tone and are appropriate to particular groups of girls on particular occasions. Detention is a punishment which is very much an extension of the personality of the mistress or prefect in charge. She is in control of it and her individuality is stamped upon it. The way she organises it, therefore, is to a large extent determined by her personal "style".

Most detentions of any length are spent in the completion of some imposition. Writing lines, of course, is the most usual and certainly a very excellent one, although other standard impositions and punitive exercises* may be set as detention work with excellent effect. Some mistresses consider making a detention class sit in silence even more effective than setting the most tedious work, and certainly we would recommend that this method be used at least occasionally. Assuming, however, that work is to be set, the question arises as to whether a certain amount of work should be finished in a detention. There are various approaches to this question. Some mistresses will set a line, for example, or some pages to copy, and simply tell the girls to work on them until the expiration of the hour or whatever the duration of the detention. Others will set a fixed number of lines, intended to fill the approximate duration and allow girls to go when they have (satisfactorily) completed them. This may mean some girls leaving early and others staying on after the end of the detention. Alternatively those who have not finished may be allowed to finish in their own time, or even be excused, since they have spent the full time in detention.

Other mistresses will set an imposition which every girl should be able to finish within the time, instructing girls to sit silently with their hands on their heads as soon as they have finished—no one being allowed to leave until the full hour has expired. An interesting variation on this, which we have encountered occasionally, is to set an amount of work which should approximately fill the time, making girls wait in silence when they have finished: however the detention does not end at a predetermined time, but when the last girl has finished her imposition. This is an extremely effective measure for adding to the frustration of a detention. The slowest girl feels utterly wretched for holding up the class, while all the others feel terribly fidgety and irritable waiting for the last girl to grind out her lines. This method has much to commend it. Practically it may add no more than five or ten minutes to the length of a detention, but psychologically it increases its effectiveness considerably, and it is of the essence of a good detention that it should be as irksome as possible to those

* See the section on punitive exercises, pp. 45-49. This important aspect of the disciplinary art should be carefully studied.

enduring it. Time, after all, is a precious commodity, and it is better to have an hour's highly effective detention than two hours' moderately effective detention.

This leads us on naturally to the question of whether a detention should be for a fixed period of time. Most detentions are for a fixed period or nearly so for the obvious reason that they must be fitted into the day's itinerary. However, there is a great psychological value in allowing a detention to "expand" beyond its allotted time, and some mistresses allow an hour for a half-hour detention, knowing that they do not intend to let the girls (or all of them) go at the end of the half-hour. This, of course, is another way of setting an hour's or three quarters of an hour's detention, but many people consider it more effective, the "extra" time being felt more acutely precisely because it is superadded.

On the other side, it may be argued that knowing from the beginning that one has a whole hour's detention ahead of one has a powerful effect in itself which is lost by the "expanding" method. Both schools of thought have their merits. Many mistresses and prefects, however, do not plan their "expansions" in quite this way, but are quite happy to regard half an hour's or an hour's detention as precisely that, and equally happy to keep girls on for considerable length of time afterwards if their work is in any way unsatisfactory, or, indeed, if the whim so takes them.

Whether a detention should be stated to be for a fixed period or "until the work be satisfactorily completed" is another fundamental decision. In favour of a "fixed period" detention is its greater practical convenience for those organising and supervising it as well as the psychological value of letting a girl realise that she is inexorably to be held until a certain time, which, in the case of the longer detentions seems, to the young mind, horribly distant. In favour of the detention which is not so precisely limited is a certain *piquance* which it lends to the work and to the occasion.

The number of lines set is then directly related to the length of time spent, and a girl knows that only by working her way through her task can she earn her release. The work must be careful enough to be accepted, but at the same time if one proceeds too slowly one's time of confinement will be considerably extended. This arrangement puts a greater pressure upon the girls than the system which allows them to relax in the confidence that whatever happens (unless the work be rejected) they will be released when the clock's hands reach a certain point, and, on the whole, if it is not inconvenient from an organisational point of view, the present authors tend to prefer it.

A combination of the two approaches is sometimes favoured, whereby the detention lasts a set time *and* a set number of lines (or other set imposition) is required. The pupil is thus penalised either if her work is untidy or unsatisfactory or if she fails to complete it within the time of the detention. Girls finishing before the end of the detention are required to sit in silence or given extra work until it is time to leave. In a detention of this sort the pupil has a double anxiety—if she works too slowly she will be punished for failing to finish by the end of the detention; if she works too hurriedly her work will be rejected for untidiness, and in some cases there may seem a very narrow channel between the Scylla and Charybdis of these two punitive eventualities, thus giving the detention a greater intensity than would otherwise be the case.

The question of "detention homework" is another one that should be considered. This is an interesting concept which we believe to be of fairly recent origin. While some mistresses regard a detention as an integral punishment in itself, others see it as a sort of punitive lesson which may, or should, have its own punitive homework tasks attached to it.

To a large extent this is an individual matter with certain mistresses being known for favouring this custom and giving rise to inward sighs among the girls as soon as they are seen to be "taking detention". In some schools the custom is established as a general rule for all but the shorter detentions, and again, in some establishments it is a mandatory part of certain detentions, being regarded as an aspect of their special character.

Detention is a highly flexible and adaptable form of discipline—it can be varied in length and in nature, it can incorporate elements of corporal discipline either as part of the detention or by means of a very strict application of the minutest rules of conduct, or by both means; the variety of different impositions itself allows one to "colour" a detention in a great variety of ways, and we would urge our readers to study the section on punitive exercises closely in order that she may not feel that lines are the only form of detention labour (although we fully recognise that these are a tried and very excellent staple).

It may be fixed or extensible; flatly tedious or electric with the atmosphere of rigour and apprehension; it may be cold and very formal, it may be dull and matter-of-fact, with the mistress or senior clearly paying no more attention to the whole affair than duty bids her pay, and with her mind firmly upon her marking or on her own prep., and while this atmosphere may be due to an entirely permissible negligence, it may also be an effect deliberately contrived which has a psychological value of its own; conversely it may be highly intimate with a feeling of every movement, every breath a shade more audible than it should be, every rustle of the paper or shuffle of the feet in changing position noticed and pounced upon*; and again, this close scrutiny may have many different tones, from the cold and forbidding to a certain warmth and delicacy of severity. The advanced mistress will be acutely aware of these *nuances* and of many more—for we have merely indicated in the broadest outline the broad range of forms, tones and colours which a detention may have, many of them, in their subtler aspects, perhaps unique to a particular mistress, even as a song may be interpreted in exactly a particular way by one singer alone—and will learn to make of this commonest form of schoolgirl discipline an instrument of the rarest delicacy and refinement.

* There is a form of detention in some schools called "Absolute Silence Detention" in which every audible sound made during the course of a girl's punitive labours is a sharply and instantly punished offence. In our view this is an institution which should be much more widely adopted.

2. Lines

The sensibility of lines — Practical merits as a form of punishment — Virtues of the set line — Length of the line Neatness & uncertainty whether work will be checked Correcting lines — The "bare glance" — Unusual awards The "Magical Thousand" — Multiples of 1,000 lines.

AMONG THOSE punishments which do not fall into the category of "corporal", the most usual takes the form of an imposition—a task, preferably lengthy and repetitive, which must be completed by the girl being thus disciplined. Among impositions—especially in schools, but also in the home, the office and elsewhere—the best known and most frequently employed is the long tried and tested, the well-beloved imposition of "lines".

The form of this punishment is so well known that it seems almost unnecessary to describe it; however for the sake of completeness, we shall do so. Essentially, the punishment may take two forms, either the setting of so many lines of poetry to be copied or, more usually, the written repetition of a sentence dictated by the mistress or prefect (we assume the scholastic setting throughout the main part of this essay as that is the one in which we have most experience of this form of discipline). It is a punishment which is too often treated in a cold and functional manner, as if it were somehow less vital and full of sensibility than, say, a spanking or a dose of the strap.

We wish to put forward most strongly the thesis that this is not so: that there may be a depth of sensibility in the imposition of lines quite as profound as that which may be found in any corporal chastisement. There is, in some respects, even a greater intensity: a more pronounced sense of ruling over the life and lib erty of the girl subjected to this discipline—of dictating, with a few lightly-spoken words, the entire course and colour of her existence in the near future. We have known the closest and most fruitful of disciplinary *rapports* to be founded partly or even largely upon the imposition of lines and are firm supporters of the extension of this form of discipline beyond the boundaries of the academy.

For a maidservant, for example, the condemnation to spend a portion of her precious leisure hours in the written repetition of some improving sentence may well be more effective on occasions than a good switching (or may be a salutary supplement to the same); for office girls, the taking home of a sheaf of foolscap to be covered with lines by the next morning is a wonderful promoter of future neatness, diligence, smartness and punctuality (they may also remain behind in the office after hours to complete the imposition, but this really comes under the heading of detention—a form of discipline which also might profitably be used more widely than its current scholastic application). Indeed, with the introduction of the Office Cane into many advanced places of business today, the use of such impositions would seem to be the logical next step—and one which would perhaps find favour among the backward-looking minority who still imagine that an occasional caning with the light-weight implement authorised by the Home Office for this purpose is in some way bad for an office-girl (it might also open their eyes to see how many girls, faced with the choice between a substantial imposition and a caning will freely choose the latter to "get it over with").

On the purely practical side, lines have the advantage of being one of the few punishments which can effectively be given *in absentia*. Where a *protégée* is separated from her mistress, effective discipline may be imposed very satisfactorily by letter or over the telephone. In this age of discipline, when the looseness of yesterday is being so roundly rejected and new areas of sensibility discovered and understood, we feel that the often-undervalued discipline of lines should be seen with fresh eyes: its delicacy and grace, its great versatility and its psychological subtlety should be appreciated by the new generation of feminine disciplinarians. The imposition of lines should be refined to a gentle art, and valued as one of the delicate and purifying things of life.

The Virtues of a Set Line

ONE OF THE beauties of this punishment is its ease and simplicity—the fact that but a moment's thought and the speaking of a few words by a mistress may condemn a child to hours of repetitive and tiresome labour. Sometimes, in order to increase this element, a "set line" or "standard line" may be established, so that the mistress is not even put to the trouble of devising a line. This system was used at S—— School at various periods. In one house the set line for the week was pinned upon the noticeboard by the housemistress, and the prefects and mistresses had merely to say to a girl "One hundred lines" and the punishment was imposed. The girl knew that she must copy the "set line" one hundred times and deliver it to the mistress's study by five o'clock the next day—the standard time for the submission of such punishments.

Of course, those in authority were always free to set their own lines, and often did so, especially if they wished to amuse the young delinquent by setting a rather longer line than the standard one, but the existence of the "set line" had a very definite effect toward increasing the amount of written punishment imposed in that house. The ease and freedom felt, especially by the prefects, in being able to say "Lydia, 100 lines", perhaps as a sort of aside, without even turning away from one's conversation with a fellow-prefect, was almost intoxicating in its bestowal of a sense of effortless power. At the same time, the younger girls stood more in awe of the prefects as an order of beings who could and would ruin an afternoon's leisure without giving the matter a minute's worth of her own attention. It was noticed also that the prefects and even the mistresses often gave larger numbers of lines than before, perhaps tiring of constantly saying "50 lines" and "100 lines" and finding it interesting to vary the refrain with "250 lines", "300 lines" and even perhaps the occasional four or five hundred.

This system was introduced and found to be of great advantage whenever one of those occasional periods of turbulence and unruliness settled upon the school or upon a particular form, year or house (all schoolteachers and governesses will be familiar with this phenomenon). It has a great effect in increasing respect for authority, calming the passions, and, indeed, in giving the children something more tranquil with which to occupy their leisure hours!

The Length of the Line

AS WELL AS THE question of the number of lines, the punishment may be varied in other ways, the most obvious of these being the length of the line. Some mistresses take a whimsical pleasure in, say, keeping a girl behind after class to receive her punishment and saying, "Well, Veronica, you are to write fifty lines for me," and even as Veronica is breathing a sigh of relief, proceeding to dictate, or to write upon the blackboard a form of words orotund and leisurely in its expression, replete with dependent clauses, causing the child's heart to sink ever more deeply as the line seems to be coming to a natural conclusion only to open into some fresh convolution of bluestocking verbosity and as it becomes apparent that the task will be as heavy as three or four hundred lines of a more usual length. Such procedures, of course, would lose their force if employed with too great a frequency, and, in any case, some mistresses never use them; but it should be considered as a means of increasing the psychological effectiveness of the punishment.

Conversely, a prefect may set the line first, giving a simple line of just a few words "I must not shout", for example, and then dash the child's hopes with an off-hand "Two hundred and fifty by tomorrow evening, please." The opposite effect may also be achieved. The girl who is noisy in the corridor may be brought up sharply with the following: "I am going to make an example of you, Fiona. You will have ample time to repent your thoughtlessness over the writing of four hundred lines." A lengthy lecture—or perhaps the leaving of the room for some time to attend to some other business—is recommended at this point. And then: "Take down the line, please: Silence is golden." This is still a substantial imposition, but the child is forcibly impressed with the thought of how much worse it might have been and doubtless will be should the offence recur, and of how wholly her fate is in the hands of her superiors.

The length of the line is often not a matter of much considered thought, and can easily become dictated by mere habit. Certain mistresses are known for mostly setting short, simple lines, probably because they are the first that pop into their heads (they probably set longer ones every now and then, when they are cross). Others dutifully compose lines of a middling length because that is what seems to them the "right" length for a punishment line, while Miss S—— is well known for the length of her lines; solid slabs of artfully constructed prose three or four lines long, even though she sets the same numbers as the other mistresses. Very probably there are one or two prefects who gleefully copy this trait, perhaps making their youthful compositions even more elaborate than those of the mistress they have suffered under. No doubt these foibles are an ineradicable part of human nature, but we wish here to express our opinion that the length of the line is, ideally, something to be considered: a part of the psychological balance of the punishment as a whole which should be so weighed as to make the punishment as elegant, effective and as appropriate to its circumstances as possible.

Neatness

THE THIRD IMPORTANT consideration in the setting of lines is neatness; some prefects and mistresses—probably the majority—will accept lines of almost any quality, others will take pleasure in rejecting a hundred lines for a few minor imperfections, demanding that they be done again and perhaps even doubling or trebling them, or bringing out the cane for the offence of "unsatisfactory completion of punishment work."

Girls quickly mark the difference between the two types, and it would be a revelation to many to compare a page of lines written by the same girl for a mistress whom she knows will accept them with a cursory glance and for a prefect who has a reputation for re-setting, doubling and strapping.

Curiously, there is often little ground between these extremes, which is unfortunate, because a girl should at least work in the realisation that her lines will be looked at. Some girls are so confident that the lines will not be checked that they deliberately do the wrong number, or even insert "amusing" variations into the lines in the middle of the imposition, on the (usually correct) assumption that only a few at the beginning or end will ever be read.

These variations are often shown to other girls before the lines are submitted in order to demonstrate the "wit" and daring of the writer. The present writer recalls one girl who "concealed" a great deal of innocent hilarity within the lines that "would never be read" and well remembers the consternation registered on the countenance of this young person upon learning that she must repeat the imposition of 150 lines every day for a fortnight, with a sharp application of between three and a dozen strokes (depending upon the excellence or otherwise of the lines) of the Junior Dormitory Cane (a light instrument, but, as the girls put it, "a real stinger") upon the reception of each repetition.

Methods of "correcting" lines are various and each has its particular charm. The simple act of tearing the lines in half or into pieces with the information that they are unsatisfactory and must be repeated is especially effective where a long imposition has been completed and sometimes has the effect of reducing a girl to tears. Some mistresses go through the imposition, scoring in red ink through each unsatisfactory line, or circling unsatisfactorily formed letters; each line thus rejected to be repeated several times—often three, five or ten times. Other mistresses may award a stroke of the strap or five minutes' detention for every rejected line. To tell a girl in advance that her imposition is to be "marked" in this way greatly increases her care and patience in writing it. The girl who has not been warned of this strict marking may be given a salutary shock as she sees the mistress, whom she had expected to receive the lines with no more than a glance, set to work closely examining them with a severe countenance and dotting the page with red marks. The simple rejection of the entire imposition with the instruction that it is now doubled—or even, occasionally, trebled—is perhaps the most devastating "correction" of all. This penalty may be awarded for lateness of presentation as well as for untidiness.

As we have suggested, the degree of severity with which an imposition is "marked" and "corrected" should be a matter for some consideration. Undoubtedly the temperament of the mistress or prefect is, and should be, a factor. Some really do not wish to concern themselves with an imposition once it is completed, and the off-hand, scarcely-noticing manner in which they accept what may represent two or three hours of girlish tedium is an important *nuance* of the punishment. Others have a sense of order and neatness which demands that lines be checked carefully.

Nonetheless, we feel that, in the interests of effective and subtly-calculated punishment, the matter should sometimes be considered. It should be borne in mind that when a girl knows that her work is to be sternly marked, fifty lines which must be written with the most painstaking care and attention may be a greater punishment than a hundred lines of the same length set in the "normal" way—a punishment which is also intensified by the psychological uncertainty as to whether the task will really be "over" when it is completed; that when she does not know it, the imposition of 100 lines which are almost certain to be rejected and repeated is psychologically very different from setting 200 lines in the first place, and 100 lines which are repeated twice and finally doubled before they are at last accepted (making 500 in all) is an entirely different sort of punishment from a straightforward imposition of 500 lines, a punishment on some occasions much better and on others not so good.

On the other hand, the fairly free acceptance of lines is not to be derided. It has its uses. Very strict marking does greatly increase the time taken up by lines, both from repetition (unless other means are used to chastise unaccepted lines) and from the much slower speed of a girl working to make each line, each word, each letter acceptable to her taskmistress. 150 lines under these circumstances, even if no correction work is necessary may be the equivalent of 300 "ordinary" lines. This is often an excellent thing, but sometimes the mistress may want the sound and feel of setting the higher numbers. She may desire the crushing effect of announcing "500 lines" without actually giving the equivalent of 1,000 or 1,500. She may want the overwhelming psychological effect of giving the dreaded "thousand lines" without prolonging the punishment to inordinate lengths. In such cases lighter marking is called for, though even here, the present writer cannot advocate the "bare glance" or automatic acceptance which is all too common.

Is there ever a case for the "bare glance"? Yes, we should say there is. As we have already indicated, it can be psychologically effective in indicating how very little the girl's punitive labours may signify to the superiors who impose them. Some mistresses and prefects are known for this and it is part of their "style"—it suits them. Others may vary their methods, and it can be particularly effective when a girl is expecting the strictest marking, to accept the lines occasionally without a glance. She has worked at them with the greatest care, extending the dreary time of her punishment to twice its normal length or more. Now her careful work does not receive even ten seconds' attention. The pages are not turned. She might have scribbled it all at breakneck speed. She might have written only half the set amount. It would not have mattered after all.

When a mistress is known for being unpredictable in her reception of impositions, an interesting tension is created in the hearts of her pupils—should one *really* work so horribly slowly and carefully when, as likely as not she will accept the work without considering it for a moment? *Dare* one risk rushing a bit when she may be in one of her "fussy moods" and examine every individual line? It is something of an unorthodox "effect", perhaps, to aim for, but one that is not without its *piquance* and charm.

Unusual Numbers

JUST AS TOO many mistresses give too little attention to the examination of lines, so they may give too little thought to the numbers they set. In a way, of course, this is often as it should be. Lines do not demand much of the setter. It is the pupil who has to think about them, write them, *live* with them until they are finished. Many mistresses set the standard "100 lines" for almost everything, occasionally venturing to two or three hundred when much displeased, and there is nothing wrong with this style.

Nonetheless, there are shades and colours that many mistresses might enrich their work by considering. Each number of lines has its own subtle feeling. "100 lines", of course, is the standard, classical imposition. "50 lines" (often set by prefects) has a feeling of lenity about it, although it is a tiresome enough imposition when one actually sets about doing it. Slightly more unorthodox numbers should sometimes be considered. 150 is a number with a gentle charm. More than the standard 100, but not yet "taking wing" into the multiples of 100. It is an interestingly homely little punishment which at once feels lenient because it has avoided the more obvious 200 and severe because it is substantially more than the standard 100. 250 is a nice, solid quantity: it has a feeling of being well-considered. It is half 500, seeming to suggest the higher reaches of punitive imposition and, while it does not yet aspire to them, the pupil will find it weighty enough. It is a good "warning" number. 350 is another number with charm. Do consider it from time to time.

Small numbers are also not without interest. Sometimes in schools where a standard line is written up for the week, the habit of giving ten, fifteen and twenty-five lines for minor offences is encouraged. Such sums are irritating rather than crushing, but they are good for maintaining order in little things and may rapidly mount up. It is a useful system to consider in some circumstances. 25 lines is a punishment which should not be neglected. It sounds light and whimsical. It is light, but not quite as light as it sounds. If you are inclined to disbelieve us, stop now, in the middle of this paragraph, and write, 25 times, "I must be a good, demure, obedient young lady." Have you done that? Then no doubt you see what we mean. 25 to 50 lines is an excellent punishment for breaking small bad habits like bad posture, bad pronunciation and so forth. The lines must be written *immediately,* every time the girl is found doing—or not doing—whatever is in question.

The Magical Thousand

FROM SMALL NUMBERS to large ones. Perhaps the most crushing phrase in the schoolmistress's repertoire is "You will take a thousand lines." There is something magical about the dreaded thousand: so utterly crushing; such a heavy, inescapable sentence that comes down upon one, changing the colour of one's immediate life. One remembers the oppressive tedium of the 100 or 200 one wrote last week, but a thousand seems almost outside comprehension. There is a curious satisfaction in imposing such a rounded, thorough punishment. From 500 onwards, lines take on a darker, more serious colouring. 600, 700, 750, 800 are numbers whose announcement leaves one numbed and a little chilled, but 1,000 brings one somehow into a new dimension of seriousness and severity. A thousand lines has something of the fateful, drastic quality of the cane in schools where the cane is rarely used and only for serious offences: something which suddenly brings the erring child up against the hard reality of Fate. The very phrase "a thousand lines" has something of the classic severity of "six of the best", and, indeed, with less whimsy and more heaviness about it.

The present writers are of the opinion that every girl should at some time endure the experience of writing a thousand lines or more. There are few, if any, who do not on some occasion deserve it, and distressing as it may be at the time, it is, in itself, a part of the education of character. We have seen many girls surprisingly improved after such a long and gruelling imposition—at once quietened and in a curious way deepened, and also somehow refreshed, as if a period of dull restriction had increased their appreciation of the simple pleasures and everyday liberties of life. As with the severer forms of discipline in general, girls vary considerably in how frequently large numbers of lines will benefit them. Some girls—probably most—require such discipline only rarely, but there are those who benefit and actually flourish under their fairly frequent application. These are not necessarily the girls who find them most tolerable; rather they are those who have an inward need for submission and the subjugation of the will to that of another. Such subjugation does not come within the compass of usual school discipline, but may sometimes flower between a mistress (or often a prefect) and a girl who have a particular *rapport.*

Conversely, it is true that some mistresses are prone to set the dreaded thousand lines more easily than others. A majority will not do it save in exceptional circumstances, but there are those who regard this form of punishment as a salutary part of regular school discipline. They will set a thousand lines not infrequently and sometimes will sentence a whole class to this crushing imposition. Their classes tend to be exceptionally quiet, subdued and well turned-out. Such mistresses will be prone to set 1,500 or 2,000 for more serious offences, and we have heard such formidable ladies speak warmly of the virtues of "a few thousand lines" for the cure of this or that fault. Such mistresses may also set a thousand lines of more than usual length: an instruction to write a long, complex sentence one thousand times is one of the most heart-oppressing that can be received.

This brings us on to the subject of multiples of a thousand. These are rare for all mistresses and all girls, only occurring in exceptional circumstances, but can be an excellent discipline in certain cases. We recall a girl who was directly defiant to a mistress who, after consideration of the matter, decided to suspend her from all lessons and to take her to every class she was teaching for the next few days, seating her always at the back of the class where she would employ her time in completing 3,000 lines which were subject to the closest scrutiny, several pages often being rejected for inadequate neatness. At the end of this ordeal (which also included several corporal chastisements) the girl's tendency to insubordination went into abeyance for a very long time. We have heard of prefects giving one, two or even three thousand lines as "holiday tasks" to their favourite juniors at the end of term. This is not a practice which is officially approved, but in our view, so long as there is a real *rapport* and the girls are not being oppressed entirely against their will (and this is not usually the case among girls, especially those brought up in the sensitive atmosphere of an advanced school), it does little harm and often much good. Spread over the period of a holiday, these large impositions are not as onerous (provided they are approached sensibly and not left to the last minute) as when given in a more concentrated form. This is generally the case with high numbers of lines. The instruction "You will present 150 lines a day for the next week" is actually an imposition of just over a thousand lines (if Sunday be included), yet it has not nearly the suffocating weight of a thousand lines to be presented in one or two days. What it lacks in immediate force, of course, it makes up in duration—the obligation to produce today's 150 lines being continually with the girl.

As we have said before, the skilful mistress will weigh the relative merits of setting the same imposition in different forms. We might even say that there is a method midway between these two. If one were to say "You will take a thousand lines" and to follow this (either immediately or at a later time) with the instruction that they may be presented in installments of 100 a day for the next ten days, one has at once the effect of setting the fateful thousand, and of giving the longer punishment, which is at once a mitigation and an extension of the suffering. A punishment such as "You will write 100 lines a day for the rest of term" is in fact likely to be an imposition of several thousand lines, but has a very different tone and character from a simple imposition of four or five thousand lines.

The unimaginative may argue that the words, or the precise form in which a punishment is set, is of no real importance, and is purely psychological, but we reply that lines are in any case a wholly psychological punishment. The suffering is "all in the mind". A girl can only ever be writing one line at any given time, and few girls would mind writing a single line in the least—it is the memory of what she has written before and the knowledge of what she has still to write which make the imposition a punishment at all. Therefore the way it is set, the perception of the punishment, is a vital part of its nature.

This also is why such questions as the length of a line, the meticulousness with which it is marked and the severity with which it is "corrected" are all vital to the "colouring" of the punishment. One hundred long lines; 200 "normal" lines; 300 very short ones; 50 lines which will be scrutinised, rejected and doubled, the new work therefore done with painstaking care and slowness—these four punishments may all take the same length of time by the clock, sitting in uniform at a desk, to complete. To the unsubtle mind they are "the same", or at any rate equivalent punishments. To the mind alive with the New Sensibility, they are four quite different things, each with its own unique flavour and *bouquet,* each appropriate to a particular combination of occasion and individual girl rather than another, each to be weighed, sensed, savoured and appreciated in its own particular way.

There are of course, a dozen variants and hybrids of these four, all of which would take up the same amount of objective disciplinary time—but by no means the same amount of subjective time, or the same *quality* of time. When we say—as we propose to say—that setting lines is an art, we are likely to be suspected of making a statement that is both *clichéd* and strictly untrue. We maintain, nonetheless, that setting lines is an art—or at any rate that it can be. A minor art to be sure, but insofar as it conveys to its "audience" a particular *nuance* of this particular aspect of the variegated human tapestry called discipline, an art by all means.

3. Other Impositions

Copying — Extra Homework — Special punitive exercises
The need for taking pains — Learning
Testing learned work

LINES ARE BY far the most favoured form of imposition, but there are numerous other types of punitive exercise which may be set, either as detention work or to be done unsupervised in a girl's spare time.

Copying

SUCH IMPOSITIONS include the copying of passages, sometimes of one passage or sometimes of the same passage more than once. A not infrequent discipline for poor presentation of work is to make a girl copy out a piece of untidy work two or three times in her fairest hand. Where there are several faults—say general untidiness, failing to underline the heading according to regulation and omitting the date, the piece might be copied out once for each fault, making, in this case, three times in all; or perhaps one might say twice or even three times for the more serious fault of general untidiness, making four or five times in all. Some mistresses favour the setting of passages to be copied in a language unfamiliar to the pupil, with, of course, severe penalties for any error. This compels her to pay the closest attention in order to copy correctly, and is a very good exercise in observation and concentration. It is not unknown for exercises of this type to be set as a discipline in the more general sense rather than a punishment. Copying, however, is usually of one's own work or of passages in one's own language or in a language which is (or should be) known to one.

Copying can sometimes be made to make the punishment fit the crime. A girl reading a novel under her desk in class or during preparation may be set to copy out the first chapter of it, or to copy out the table of contents ten times. A girl who has not learned a poem correctly may have to copy it out, perhaps once for each error in her recital. Occasionally a girl who has produced a very poor essay may be made to copy a classmate's well-composed essay two or three times, or to copy out the three essays which received the highest marks. A girl awaiting a caning might be set to copy several times some part of the section of this book which deals with the cane—the first paragraph, for example. In a case like this one may prefer not to give her the book to copy from, so the paragraph might be dictated, and only when the dictation was complete would the mistress say: "You will make ten copies of the passage you have just written, in your fairest hand. When you have completed them, you will receive your caning. If the work is not up to what I judge to be your highest standard you will receive extra strokes."

The variety of copying impositions which may be devised by an imaginative mistress is virtually unlimited, and it is hardly to be wondered at that many mistresses are very fond of them. As with other punishments, different forms of copying have different shades of sensibility. The copying of one's own untidy work has a particular feeling which is rather different from that of copying a set passage. Copying another girl's work carries with it a special kind of reproof and humiliation. This is most marked when one knows the girl to be of lesser—or no greater—ability than oneself, but that she has worked harder. On the other hand, copying the work of a girl of greater ability, whom one perhaps admires, can be inspiring and can genuinely help with one's style and with showing how one might go about such essays. Many mistresses hold that copying a short or moderate-length passage several times is a more effective discipline than copying a longer one once, even though the amount of writing may be the same. The feeling of completing the sub-task and having to begin it again adds greatly to the psychological effect of the punishment.

Extra Homework

THE LINE BETWEEN punitive exercises and the dryer sort of regular academic exercise is a fine one—often there is none at all, except that the punitive exercise is in addition to other exercises and will take up time which would otherwise have been the pupil's own. Extra homework is a favoured punishment among many mistresses, and here the only specifically punitive element lies in the quantity of work set. For example the class may have been doing quadratic equations and all girls are required to complete examples 6 to 25 in the book for homework. However Jane and Emily, who have been passing notes to each other during the lesson, will take extra homework, and must do examples 6 to the end of the exercise, which contains fifty examples in all.

Punitive exercises, while they may simply consist of an increase in ordinary set work, tend to concentrate upon the duller aspects of work. Learning irregular verbs or lists of dates, for example. Indeed, this kind of imposition may occupy an intermediate position between punitive work and academic work. Extra homework may be set simply because a girl is doing less well than she ought to in her studies. As work it will help her to improve, and at the same time she knows that she *must* improve if she does not wish to spend twice as long on her homework in the subject—and on the dullest aspects of it at that. It is an excellent device for making a girl decide that it is more tiresome to cut corners than to work diligently. Some mistresses impose extra homework more or less automatically when work drops below a certain standard. Extra homework may also take the form of more specifically punitive exercises, and any of the exercises discussed below might be given under the rubric of extra homework or extra prep.

Special Punitive Exercises

ALTHOUGH PUNITIVE work may be simply an increase in regular work, some exercises are specially designed to have a punitive character. These may be quite straightforward textbook exercises which are set in such a way that they are made particularly tedious and drawn out. Many mistresses are adept at the art of drawing out a simple exercise, and often a punitive exercise is written down for use by other mistresses in detentions and for imposition.

The expansion of a simple exercise is not a difficult matter, especially for the mistress with a dry, precise turn of mind. A simple expansion is that, in a list of questions, each question must be written out before it is answered and then virtually included in the answer. So that a comprehension question may read: "6) What animal did Sally see on her way home from school?" Normally the child might be expected to write simply: "*6) A donkey.*" Under this dispensation, however, she must write:

> *6) What animal did Sally see on her way home from school?*
> *Sally saw a donkey on her way home from school.*

When there are several questions in the exercise, and more than one exercise is set, the work becomes rather tedious. Of course, even this is not strictly a punitive exercise. Some more advanced mistresses will insist on exercises often or always being done in this fashion, and probably a majority of modern schoolmistresses will insist on the second part, i.e. *"6) Sally saw a donkey on her way home from school"* rather than *"6) A donkey."* This is in line with modern educational theory which encourages decorum and precision rather than haste and corner-cutting.

It is also important that children should be disciplined to work carefully and painstakingly rather than doing only the parts which seem interesting or even immediately useful. This is the precise opposite of the old and disastrous notion that a child must be constantly interested in her work—a recognition of the fact that submission to the mistress's particular methods and a careful carrying out of a duty is strengthening to the will and the character. Perhaps more importantly yet in the education of girls, such exercises are a training in doing all things in a decorous and pleasing manner rather than merely in the way that seems to be the shortest route to a vulgarly utilitarian goal.

Of course, much of the work done in our modern educational system is highly interesting and absorbing. Intelligent girls are stretched to capacity, and as a result their minds are alive and full of the keenest interest in a wide range of subjects. The academic standards of our schools are at a level which would have seemed little short of miraculous to a late 20th century schoolmistress (though much less so to one from the first half of that century), while girls of lesser capacity are not forced to stay at school beyond the age of fourteen when they may go into service or other suitable occupations.

The great irony is, that in the days when every effort was made to interest children in schoolwork, boredom was almost universal, while today, when the idea of pandering to mere inclination has been firmly rejected, a lively, intelligent interest in schoolwork of all sorts is the norm: and, of course, since the intellectual standards are so much higher, the work is actually more interesting in a fundamental way that no mere dressing-up or gimmicry can achieve. Instead of being saturated with low, sensationalist and wholly passive entertainment which jades the palate and maintains the attention at the lowest level, which is superficially most accessible, but ultimately incapable of maintaining real interest or satisfaction, the modern girl has the deep appreciation and interest which comes only of giving of oneself and actively putting effort and intelligence into life in order to get interest and satisfaction out of it. With work being genuinely interesting and the capacity for attention heightened rather than artificially depressed, school has become a much more stimulating place than it was in the late 20th century or in the early part of this.

Nonetheless, modern educationalists and schoolmistresses recognise an actual need for a certain portion of schoolwork to be painstaking and dry. This is partly because such work is an excellent exercise for the attention and the will, and partly because a child values her interesting work more highly if she has some experience of work which is mundane: just as modern children who are relatively rarely given sweets and cinema treats take the greatest pleasure in them, while children of an earlier generation, who ate sweets daily and sat in front of the "television" for hours on end, appreciated neither. Many spent much of their time sitting in front of one of the old home television-sets, dressed in sloppy, clown-like clothes, watching entertainments of an unbelievably low mental, moral and elocutionary level, eating sweets or "crisps" or drinking sweet, aerated drinks from tin cans—passively stimulated simultaneously through eyes, ears and mouth by every resource at the command of a rich and decadent society, and bored beyond endurance.

Quite naturally, the normal course of school work provides for a great deal of the necessary "ballast" of pedestrian labour, but it is increasingly accepted that a certain degree of deliberately painstaking work is necessary, especially for girls. The sense of working with what, from a utilitarian point of view, is unnecessary patience and fussiness at the behest of a mistress, is beneficial in cultivating obedience, meticulousness and a sweet, maidenly submission of the will. Thus, the exercises indicated above, and many others like them, are considered an excellent part of ordinary school work and not necessarily punitive at all. Once again we see the close connexion between the concept of discipline in its general sense and in the more limited sense of punishment.

Nonetheless exercises like these can be wholly punitive under certain circumstances. The particular exercise we have been discussing, for example, would normally be given to quite young children; however, as a punitive exercise it might be set to a girl of fourteen or even eighteen—it is for her devoid of any academic value, but is merely a writing-task, and one that is somewhat humiliating in that it is clearly a small child's task.

There are also many ways of making the task more irksome yet: for example, the title of the exercise may be written as a preface to each question, with all numbers written in full and prefaced by the word "number" so the girl may have to write:

Sally and Susie, Comprehension Test, Exercise number three, question number six: What animal did Sally see on her way home from school? Sally saw a donkey on her way home from school.

Or even:

Junior school English, Book number one, Chapter number seven, (page numbers thirty-two to thirty-six), Sally and Susie, Comprehension Test, Exercise number three, question number six: What animal did Sally see on her way home from school? Sally saw a donkey on her way home from school.

If the exercise contains, say, fifteen questions, the task will become quite tiresome, and if three or four exercises are set an amusingly frustrating imposition is created. The charm of this sort of thing is that any mistress can devise such exercises with the least difficulty, using any standard school textbook, and there is a great psychological value in first setting the exercise, then explaining in elaborate detail (probably with an example on the blackboard) exactly how the questions are to be written out, and then, perhaps, finishing with the final flourish: "You will then proceed to do the next three exercises in the same manner."

Exercises of this sort are splendid for detention work and extra homework as well as for impositions, and may very effectively be given to a whole class which has been unruly or inattentive, or to that portion of it which has been told to remain behind after the others have been dismissed.

Other, more purely punitive exercises are easily devised. Two which are frequently given by a mathematics mistress of our acquaintance in detentions and as extra homework are as follows:

1. Write out multiplication tables in longhand, e.g. *"When three is multiplied by one the answer is three. When three is multiplied by two the answer is six" &cetera.* Any number of tables may be set up to the full table from 1 x 1 to 12 x 12.

2. Give the child a list of long numbers (without commas) e.g. 4567089; 2479123 etc. Her task is to write out the numbers in longhand, thus "*Four million, five hundred and sixty-seven thousand and eighty-nine. Two million, four hundred and seventy-nine thousand, one hundred and twenty-three*", *&cetera.*

A variant on this imposition is to give a child a page or an exercise from her mathematics text book with the instruction not to do the work thereon, but simply to write out, in her fairest hand, a report of all the numbers which appear thereon. A page of long division or long multiplication containing a lot of long numbers is excellent for this purpose.

Such a report would take the following form: "*The first number to appear on this page is the number thirty-six. The second number to appear on this page is the number four million, two hundred and twenty-four thousand, six hundred and forty-nine*", *&cetera.* Of course, the formula of the report can be made more wordy if required, though we feel that the writing-out of numbers is the essence of this exercise★.

With all written impositions, the degree of neatness and the rigour with which they are inspected and further punishment imposed for unsatisfactory work may vary. In many cases this is a

★ The mistress from whom we had this exercise adds: "Incidentally, many girls omit to include the *page number* in their report. When they do I invariably declare the exercise incomplete and order it to be repeated."

very important aspect of the punishment and we strongly recommend the reader to study the passage on neatness in the section concerning lines* in relation to the impositions discussed in this chapter.

Learning

THE MAIN FORM of unwritten imposition consists of learning. This may take the form of the memorisation of irregular verbs, dates, poems or passages of literature; all of these come under the rubric of rote-learning. One may also require a girl to study very closely a chapter from a book which contains a large number of facts and to be able to answer any question on the chapter.

Neither form of learning, of course, is specifically punitive. Rote-learning is an important aspect of modern education. In the learning of languages it is indispensable, and to have a mind well stocked with exquisite poetry is one of the best foundations for a high sensibility and a cultivated soul. The act of learning in itself is a splendid training for the mind, the will, the powers of concentration and the memory. The punitive aspect of learning consists in its being additional to normal requirements (being set as detention-work, extra homework or an imposition) and, usually, in an additional disciplinary element in the form of punishment for mistakes.

We would advocate that this extra element of discipline be always present and prominent, in order clearly to differentiate punitive learning from ordinary learning. Rote-learning is a regular and healthy activity which most unspoiled girls enjoy, and should be encouraged to enjoy. They should not be taught to regard it as a punishment in itself. With punitive learning, the testing is the specifically punitive element. A traditional form of testing is that a girl be instructed to hold out her hand, as for a punishment, and recite the poem she has learned. The mistress or senior girl testing her holds a light classroom-type switch †—it should be light, as a considerable number of strokes may sometimes be given during this process. For each minor mistake or undue hesitation she makes, the pupil will receive a stinging

* See pp. 35– 38.

† A thin natural switch is highly recommended for this purpose. See page 70 *et seq.*

stroke across the palm; for more serious mistakes she will receive several strokes and be instructed to begin the recitation again. Normally she will not change hands after each stroke as is common in formal corporal punishment, but may be allowed to change from time to time as one hand becomes sore, if she is doing badly with her recitation. It is common for more mistakes than normal to be made due to nervousness and the pressure of the occasion. This is a legitimate part of the punishment as well as a good training in concentration under adverse conditions, from which every girl will benefit. In detentions, this testing may be carried out at intervals, helping to create a strict punitive atmosphere.

When the learning is set as an imposition it will of course be tested at the time when the child is instructed to report. Some senior girls have a habit of postponing the testing once or more times, and then announcing it suddenly, forcing the girl to continue studying her poem (or whatever it may be) if she wishes to pass her test in reasonable comfort. There is something to be said for this practice, capricious as it may seem, as it induces the girl to learn properly and not merely "cram" for a single recitation.

There are other means of testing learned work in a punitive manner. A mistress may note the number of mistakes without interrupting the recitation—it is a good idea to give a full mark for a wrong word or a long hesitation, a half-mark for stumblings and short hesitations and two marks for more serious mistakes—and then award a punishment based upon that number. The poem may be copied out once for each full mark, for example, or, if it seems more appropriate (where the poem is long or mistakes expected to be plentiful) one stanza for each full mark. Obviously the marks may be translated into punishment in numerous other ways, and, indeed, seeing a mistress impassively making a note of each error or stumbling, and having no idea what these marks may signify for one's fate is a charming little discipline in itself.

We have heard of senior girls making a junior recite in a bending-over position and applying the strap for each error. This method clearly lacks the dignity apposite to an adult punishment, and in any case is poor practice because elocution is severely impaired when the pupil is not upright.

4. Other Non-Corporal Punishments

Order Marks — As extra punishment — Standing apart Other banishments — Hands on heads — Deprivations.

MANY SCHOOLS and some governesses have a system of Order Marks which may be awarded for a variety of faults. An order mark is given when the offence is not considered serious enough for a punishment in itself, or in place of a light punishment. Some mistresses do not favour light punishments and prefer to give order marks which will add up to a "real" one. Some mistresses give them in order to avoid giving punishments—sometimes two or three at a time in order that the girl will be punished but that the mistress awarding the order marks does not have the responsibility of punishing her. This is not to be encouraged, although in the case of some older mistresses who may have had half a lifetime's conditioning against healthy disciplinary attitudes it may be understandable. Order Marks are translated into other forms of punishment—usually detention or the strap, the former being commonest.

The way in which this happens varies from school to school, and governess to governess. In some cases a child must report for punishment when she has collected three (or sometimes five) order marks. Sometimes the three must be collected in the same week for a punishment to be given—this may seem rather lenient but it does have some merit. The girl who has two Order Marks by Tuesday may be as good as gold for the rest of the week to avoid getting the third, especially if the statutory punishment is quite a severe one. Another system does not require girls to report when they have collected a set number, but has an accounting of Order Marks at the end of the week. Rather than having a fixed Order Mark penalty, the punishment will vary according to how many marks have been collected—an example would be: twenty minutes' detention for one; half an hour and three strokes of the strap for two; an hour and six strokes of the strap for three; an hour and a half and eight strokes of the strap for four; Saturday afternoon detention and one stroke of the cane on each hand for five; one thousand lines, preceded by twelve strokes of the strap and followed by two strokes of the cane on each hand for six; Saturday afternoon detention, detention every day for a week and six of the best for seven, and so on. Obviously the higher numbers are rare, but the severity of the punishments help to keep consistent bad behaviour in check. As the tally passes four, any girl but the hardiest madcap tends to restrain her behaviour for the remainder of the week.

In some systems again, Order Marks are given as an addition to all other punishments, or all but the most minor, varying in number according to the severity of the punishment; so a girl receiving a classroom strapping might also take an Order Mark. If the classroom cane was used or she was sent to Long Detention it might be two. These marks mean that every transgression leaves its stain on the girl's record. This is based on a psychological characteristic of girls which we believe is much less common among boys. Many girls regard the shame of receiving an Order Mark as being even more serious than the punishment and try very hard to avoid getting them altogether. In some schools these Order Marks given "alongside" punishments merit further punishment later, but more often they are simply a record of the fact that the girl needed punishment. Some schools offer girls a choice of retaining their Order Marks on the record or having a further punishment to "wipe them clean". Even when the punishment is a severe one—and even when the record is simply a private tally which will never be seen by parents or any one else; which may not even be retained by the school after the end of term—it is quite usual for a girl to choose to accept it and clean away the unsightly marks from the private diary of her heart.

Standing Apart

ANOTHER FAMILIAR punishment is that of standing a child in the corner of the room, or facing a wall. This is usually done only to quite small children, but may at times be effectively employed on older ones. Some mistresses prefer to make a girl stand on her chair, perhaps with her hands on her head, while the class proceeds. This is a very exposed and embarrassing position for an older girl (though younger children may well prefer it to standing in the corner). Or she may stand on a chair at the front of the class, either facing the class or facing the wall.

These positions have also a strong psychological effect. The girl feels so conspicuous and has so profound a consciousness of her removal from the ordinary course of events—she is no longer permitted to do the work that was, a moment ago, her inescapable lot—that she cannot but wonder what will be done with her at the end of the lesson.

This, of course, may vary according to the mistress's intuition from allowing the shock to be enough and showing lenience, to imposing some exemplary discipline. At the least she should be made to borrow a classmate's book and copy up the work she has missed, and if this discipline should be necessary a second time, severe chastisement should be given afterwards. Such punishment is particularly effective in cases where a girl seems disaffected from her work in general or from a particular subject—whispering, reading under the desk, not paying attention, generally doing anything rather than give her mind to the work under consideration. It is a punishment which shows her that if she really does not wish to take part in the lesson, then she may indeed be prevented from doing so. Standing on her chair, feeling alone and conspicuous, wondering what fate awaits her, she will quickly begin to wish that she were sitting down working alongside her companions, and develop a definite affection for the quotidian comfort of classroom life, however dull it may occasionally seem. It is for this reason that, while we are not advocates of undue leniency, we suggest that a mild rebuke with no further penalty can be a very effective method. The child feels suddenly restored to her old standing; she is grateful; she may well improve dramatically. If not, the punishment should be repeated with a much less gentle conclusion.

Yet another variant on this punishment is to make a girl stand outside the door. This has an even stronger effect of making her feel "banished" from everyday life. It is less conspicuous, however, than standing on a chair and one is out of sight of the mistress. It is possible, in some cases, where a girl is quite hardened or really dislikes a particular lesson, that she will not much mind—we heard of a case once in which a girl was "banished" for an indefinite period to the library which happened to be next door to her classroom and told that she might not return until she apologised. She was quite happy reading books there and never did apologise. The mistress had eventually to "forget" her edict and bring her back. This happened, needless to say, in the late 20th century, when other forms of discipline were rare: but it is an indication of the alteration in the moral state of children which is wrought by the absence of real discipline. We have heard of late-20th-century girls, in a school where Order Marks brought no further penalties, but were "a punishment in themselves", having an "Order Mark Race": actually competing to see who could accumulate the most Order Marks. This contrasts sharply with those modern girls who will accept quite severe chastisement in order to cleanse their record of Order Marks.

"Moral discipline", that is discipline where no punitive measures are used, can be very effective upon occasion, *but it can only work in an atmosphere where good discipline is already established as the norm*, and this can only be established by the use, where it is needed, of punitive discipline.

To return to our point of departure—the discipline of sending a girl to stand outside the room. As in so many cases, a mistress must use her judgement. For some girls this is a very salutary punishment; for others, in itself, it is not—but may well be if done in a baleful manner which ensures that much of the time will be spent in wondering what fate awaits at the end of the lesson.

Another aspect of this punishment, sometimes exploited very sensibly by mistresses who are particularly mild, is that a girl standing in the corridor is, in many schools, apt to be discovered by another mistress, and her time of exile may be spent starting at every sound and wondering "What if Miss T—— finds me? What will happen then?" This feeling is rendered particularly acute by the knowledge most girls have that the more advanced and stern mistresses are often both protective of the milder ones and eager to correct their excesses of leniency. We may add that the idea of sending a girl out of the class for several lessons, perhaps until she apologises or until the mistress considers her apology and her promise of amendment sufficiently sincere to be accepted, is not in itself a bad one. It is simply that a library is too comfortable a place of banishment. Standing outside the class or on a chair, most girls would quickly wish to be re-admitted, and a longer period of banishment may be just what is needed to make a bored and fractious girl positively long for the opportunity to do the work and have the lessons she had formerly disliked.

The most striking form of standing apart of which we have heard is that of sending a girl to stand in the middle of the playground where she may be overlooked by the mistress from the window. Here her disgrace may be observed by much of the school and may well lead to awkward interviews with her housemistress, dormitory prefect or other authorities as well as making her a figure of generally unwanted attention. This punishment should be used judiciously. On highly sensitive girls one should think very carefully before employing it, and on young exhibitionists, who may take a perverse pleasure in it, one should avoid it altogether, but in some cases it can be very effective and may be just the thing needed to quell a phase of defiance.

Punishments of this sort are less effective outside schools and institutions, though corner-standing and even chair-standing can sometimes be used in the home. When used in institutions the mistress must bear in mind (as every good mistress will) that such punishments isolate a girl from her companions. They are to be used when a girl is already isolating herself by a spirit of rebellion or is in danger of leading those companions in a wrong direction. Its only aim is to restore her to her class and her companions in a renewed spirit of harmony, friendship and obedience.

Hands on Heads

THIS IS REALLY a variant of the punishment above. A girl may be instructed to put her hands on her head and may be left in that position for any length of time desired. Usually this will be quite a short time—say five minutes—as this is a less drastic measure than standing her on her chair or outside the room. It is not so isolating, but still produces the same effect and the same sensations in miniature. With young children it is quite common, but with older children it is effective precisely because of its juvenile associations, and is especially good for the girl who thinks too much of herself and is a ringleader of other girls.

Occasionally it may be used for an unexpectedly long time, perhaps making the girl wonder if she has been forgotten. It should be noted that this position, if held for any length of time, turns into something of a physical discipline, as it becomes increasingly uncomfortable. Sometimes a whole class may be told to put their hands on their heads—a good punishment, for example, when a mistress returns to a noisy disorderly classroom. She may leave them in that position for a little time. She may leave the room again telling them to sit still and silent in her absence with their hands on their heads, or she may single out the worst offenders, perhaps telling them to stand and dealing with them one by one with the strap or classroom cane while the others remain seated, hands on heads; or she may simply tell them what their punishments are to be, give them impositions or put them down for detention, making a leisurely process of it, writing down the punishments and generally keeping the class in uncomfortable suspension and in an increasing sensibility of the utter subjection of the group to the whim of the individual mistress. It is an excellent exercise in the restoration of order and control.

Some mistresses and seniors like to make a girl put her hands on her head in any intervals during another punishment—say, while waiting for her lines to be set, between completing the lines and receiving her caning and so forth. This position emphasises her marionettish subordination to her mistress, and an advanced mistress may sometimes use it on occasions which are not punitive—for example she may make girls stand with their hands on their heads during dormitory inspections, particularly if the class has a bad record for tidiness. The practice of using this posture for uniform inspections is not encouraged as clothes do not sit well with the arms raised.

Deprivations

VARIOUS LONGER-TERM punishments may consist of deprivations of various sorts including loss of privileges. At schools and institutions "gating" is perhaps the most usual of these—a girl who is gated may not leave the school or college premises for the period of her punishment. At home a child's pocket money may be stopped for a stated period (usually this is to pay for some damage the child has done). Some schools operate a system of fines for certain offences. We do not recommend this for a number of reasons—in the first place a fine is a punishment which falls very unevenly on different children. A fine of, say 6d may be a very great loss to a child from a less well-off family, or merely one which does not believe in giving children much money, while to another child a fine of half a crown may mean very little. Immature children can sometimes attribute motives of cupidity to school authorities imposing fines upon them, and while this is absurd, it is better that such thoughts should not colour the atmosphere and that discipline should not only be disinterested but be seen to be disinterested. We would say, at the risk of sounding hackneyed, that money is a sordid subject. It must necessarily impinge upon all our lives, young and old, at various points, but the discipline of children and young ladies is, as we have hoped to convey, a noble thing and it is better in our view that it be kept pure of all taint of the grosser matter of this world.

Deprivations in the area of food should be considered carefully. Growing children require nourishment, and while going without a meal now and again will do little harm, it should not be overdone. Sometimes when a long imposition is set, or a detention extended from a half-holiday afternoon into the evening, tea may be missed, but normally a light supper should be allowed before bed. A child who is overweight may have food restrictions imposed (probably as a discipline for some offence but in the knowledge that this form of discipline will be felt and will be of benefit in other ways). Forbidding puddings after meals is a not uncommon deprivation, and the forbidding of all sweets can be effective, but can only be enforced at home or with an honourable girl (and most girls today are honourable) since it is all too easy to obtain sweets from other children at school.

Imposing an earlier bedtime, forbidding treats such as the cinema, withdrawing permission to use the gramophone, or (in the case of older girls) the telephone are among the many other deprivations and curtailments of privilege which may be used. Older girls who are inclined to be precocious may be forbidden to wear any clothes except school uniform (and nightclothes) at any time.

Part Two
CORPORAL PUNISHMENT

5. Spanking

Excellent for maidservants — Rare use in schools
Methods — Suitable implements — Positions and other conditions — Types of spanking — Dignity in discipline.

SPANKING MAY BE regarded as the most fundamental form of corporal punishment—indeed, the most fundamental form of punishment altogether. For most of us the first experience of punishment will have been over the knee of mother or nurse—an experience which carries with it a sensation of warmth and security as well as of strictness, and it is a double security: the security at once of being loved and looked after and of living in a world with definite bounds and limits which may not be transgressed. Both are vital to the healthy psychological development of a growing child.

Spanking is an excellent discipline for maidservants, especially ladies' maids and maids in the single-servant household which is becoming so much more common in suburban areas. Such maids often have a close and intimate relationship with the mistress, who is, in some respects, much like a mother. One should not be afraid to cane the maid when it seems necessary, but a good spanking will suffice for most disciplinary purposes and is entirely appropriate to the warmth of the mistress-servant relationship which is so much a part of the kinder, more human outlook of the New Sensibility as opposed to the older cold-cash relationship. Especially in these days when girls who are not of an academic bent may leave school at the age of fourteen to go into service, just as boys may go into apprenticeships, spanking is an ideal discipline for a young maidservant, which, while keeping her strictly up to the mark will also help her to feel cared for and at home. A maid who stays with the family may possibly go on being spanked well into adult life. Sensitivity is required here. For some girls it would not be appropriate, but for many it is an integral part of the warmth and security of a life in service; a blessing—one might almost say a "human right"—which was denied to all by the chilly commercial-political "personal independence" of earlier generations, but which is coming to be recognised as indispensable to the psychic health of many people.

Despite its popularity in the home, spanking is not much practised in schools and public institutions other than those dealing with very young children. There are exceptions. Some girls' schools include spanking as a formal punishment, especially for dormitory as opposed to classroom offences—a special slipper is sometimes kept for the purpose; while in many schools senior girls carry out unofficial spankings with hand, slipper or hairbrush, upon the hinder parts of their erring juniors.

We declare ourselves in favour of spanking in schools. It should not, of course, replace the more serious sanctions such as the cane; but it has many virtues. It is a warm, homely punishment which makes a girl feel looked after, yet at the same time it can be a very effective form of discipline. For certain girls at certain times it can be of incalculable benefit to employ a spanking rather than (or sometimes as well as) some other form of discipline. The girl who is new to the school and does not seem to settle as other girls do may become fractious and need a lot of discipline—yet the coldness and formality of detentions and strappings punctuated by the stark rigour of the cane, may simply compound all her hostile feelings about school, making her more intractable than ever. Of course, on the one hand, one cannot simply be lenient with her for that reason in a soft, 20th-century manner, and on the other hand one should not lose sight of the fact that some girls—a small minority—are genuinely unsuited to school life (to boarding school life, at any rate), and we are firmly of the opinion that such girls, after a good trial period of a full term, should be put under a governess or sent to a day-school. However, such girls *are* a small minority, and in most cases, with sensitive and firm handling, the "misfit" will begin to settle in.

Here, in our view, is a classic case for spanking. If the girl's housemistress is not of the sympathetic, motherly type, then one should find a mistress who is to take charge of her more serious discipline—one that is, who while being sympathetic is by no means "soft". Needless to say the course she pursues will be a delicate and individual one, and we are by no means putting forward spanking as a panacea, but the use of spanking as a discipline during this period may well be less alienating than more formal methods, although we do not suggest that the girl should be immune from other punishment.

This is an extreme case where spanking may be called for, but there are others. Some girls who are by no means normally unsettled may respond to it well under certain circumstances. School matrons sometimes use it, and some mistresses and housemothers consider spanking to suit their maternal "style".

Again, for the tense and highly-strung girl, perhaps given to boisterous excesses which are alien to the gentleness of her inner nature, punishment is sometimes considered a good in itself, helping her to relax, to feel gentle, sweet and subdued. Such girls are frequently extremely sensitive to punishment, although it is very necessary for them. Spanking is often exactly the right medicine; sometimes very gentle spanking which helps to calm her and win her confidence, in many cases mounting in severity as the punishment proceeds and as she becomes ready for each successive stage of pain (in a close *rapport* she may even ask for it). Such punishment may build up her nervous tolerance to punishment, allowing her, as time goes on, to take increasingly severe whippings.

Of course such "leading in" is not usually appropriate when it is a question of severe discipline for some particularly bad offence (though there are those who favour a gentle "building up" even to this, holding that discipline, while it may be severe, should as far as possible retain the willing assent of the child); but it is increasingly recognised by child psychologists and others that, in the case of a certain minority of children, discipline is not merely a deterrent and corrective but serves a therapeutic purpose in itself. Obviously such "medicinal discipline" should only be given in cases where there is a close understanding between the child (or indeed the adult woman, for this is not necessarily restricted to children) and the disciplinarian, but to ignore its potentialities is to close the door to an important therapeutic technique and to condemn many nervous and wounded souls to needless mental suffering. The line between discipline and therapy in such cases is clearly a delicate one (many experts hold that it would lose its effectiveness if the disciplinary aspect was entirely absent), and spanking, with its highly intuitive and sympathetic nature, while it is by no means the only form of punishment which can be so used, is likely to form the basis of "therapeutic discipline" especially in its early stages.

At the opposite extreme from the delicate girl who requires spanking is the overly-independent young miss who takes lines, the strap and even the occasional caning very much in her stride in a rather boyish manner. For such a girl a really good spanking may be just the proper remedy: it will offend her pride and her sense of independence, and, if properly executed, will hurt her much more than she expects. If she can be brought to tears over a mistress's knee or that of a senior girl (perhaps in public, or in private but with the threat of a public demonstration at a later date), a great deal of the air will be taken out of her, as her classmates might put it.

Spanking, then, has many uses. It should not be neglected as an aid to school discipline, and even if it is used but rarely it should be kept in reserve as a possibility for some occasions. Schools which have taken it up as a regular discipline have often reported favourably upon its effectiveness.

Methods of Spanking

MANY IMPLEMENTS may be used for spanking, but in this country only three are common in formal use, viz. the hand, the slipper and the hairbrush. Purpose-made tapettes or spanking-paddles, usually made of wood or leather, can be purchased and some schools have them, but while they are common enough in Europe and in America, they have not yet become popular in this country. Perhaps if spanking continues to make headway as a formal school punishment they will become more widespread.⋆

In the home, wooden spoons, spatulas and other household implements have been pressed into service with great effect; how-

⋆ Since this was written leather paddles in particular have become much more common, especially in the home.

ever, while these are entirely appropriate for the use of servants they may be considered a little too homely for the mistress of the house. Senior girls in schools, either because they are not given the use of official implements, or impelled by the quest for novelty, have been known to use a remarkable variety of implements from flat lengths of wood to fives bats and even ping-pong racquets. Canes and straps (except the tiny nursery cane) cannot and should not be used for spanking.

For formal use, though, as we have said, only three implements are at all widely used—the hand, the slipper and the hairbrush, although one can deliver an effective spanking with an eighteen-inch ruler. The hand can be used quite effectively, especially upon the unprotected flesh above the level of the stockings and below that of the knickers. Those who are really expert at this mode of punishment can make it sting more than one might expect, but despite its strongest advocates we are obliged to record that hand-spanking can only ever come into the category of mild to moderate punishment (the only possible exception being when it is employed after some other punishment on already-chastised parts).

This being said, we must also state that spanking with the other usual implements, the slipper and the hairbrush, need by no means be the rather gentle punishment it is usually considered by those who neither give nor receive it. A sound spanking, well administered, can be a very salutary punishment.

The slipper can take a number of forms. There are delicate bedroom slippers which are really too flimsy for the job. A good leather or rubber-soled slipper is required, though it need by no means be ungainly. A fine lady's slipper with a hard leather sole can combine a dainty appearance with an unremitting sting.

The hairbrush will normally be wooden. Silver or other metals are impossible, though we have seen an ivorite hairbrush used to good effect. It should have a flat back and should not be too small. Those charming wooden clothes-brushes which look like large hairbrushes are splendid, and perhaps better than the hairbrush itself. The heavier hardwoods, like ebony, can tend to bruise. We do not oppose their use on all occasions, but a light to medium-weight wood gives the stinging smack that is required.

The usual position for spanking is over the knee. With small children this is very simple. They fit neatly on the lap. With a larger girl one may sit on a chair and put her over in the conventional manner (she may well touch the floor with both feet and hands), one may choose a sofa, allowing her upper body to rest along its length, or one may use the position most favoured by senior girls in schools. One sits well back on a bed, in about the middle and the girl lies over one's lap. Essentially she is lying face down on the bed with her seat raised by one's knees.

Spankings (that is beatings with slipper, hairbrush, paddle *&c.* which have the essential quality of spankings) can also be given with the girl over a desk or lying on a bed with oneself sitting or standing beside her. The essential quality of spankings will be described fully in the last section of this chapter, but we should say that an over-the-desk spanking, as opposed to a more formal punishment, is one in which the number of strokes is not declared in advance, are not necessarily all of equal force and there is a greater degree of intimacy. The mistress or senior may well hold the girl down by placing her free hand on her back and pressing her to the desk, a pressure at once restrictive and comforting.

One may punish over the skirt (in which case the girl must be well bent and a reasonably heavy implement must be used), over the petticoat or on the seat of the knickers and the unprotected thighs.

If you have the girl over your knee in any of the positions indicated, you cannot use the same force as if you were standing up. Remember this and put real vitality into your strokes. Let the implement strike home with a loud, satisfying slap and feel its force vibrate through the girl's body to your own. A spanking can be a somewhat underrated punishment, so let her know from the beginning that you mean business.

Types of Spanking

SPANKING IS A highly sensitive and variable punishment. It stands virtually at the antipodes from caning, in which a set and limited number of strokes are administered, each one to be of maximum value. A spanking is very rarely limited as to the number of strokes. It is a long punishment, the longest of corporal punishments, and each stroke may be shaped by the instinct of the moment. There are brisk, hard spankings with a stinging leather sole; slow, heavy spankings with a large hairbrush: there are long, mild spankings and short ferocious ones and interminable, severe ones which pass from tears to silent suffering to tears again.

The "average" or "normal" spanking stroke is a hard, resounding one which causes a considerable sting. In itself it is rather more bearable than a stroke of the strap, but the punishment lies in the accumulation. A spanking may go on—and on—and on. There may be periods during a long spanking when the strokes are relatively mild, merely maintaining the rhythm and the soreness while the child recovers herself a little. There may be gentle strokes that are hardly strokes at all, and then there may be Victorian strokes—great, full-blooded slaps that make one tingle with pain. Many mistresses like to give a dozen or more of these to round off any spanking.

A spanking is, in many ways, something like a conversation, or even a song. A long, wordless but intense and passionate communication takes place.

Sometimes, for a long and complex spanking, more than one implement is used, the mistress changing from the strong, penetrating strokes of the heavy hairbrush to the sharp sting of the light leather slipper and back again, perhaps interspersing a dose of the ruler for variety. This may seem whimsical, but a mistress finely attuned to her *protegée* will know the exact moment to change implements, the different "voices" of the punishment (represented both by different implements and by different sorts and rhythms of stroke from the same one) weaving in and out like the parts of a string quartet.

Other spankings are simply severe: more like canings in tenor, and yet, of course very different. There are the feared mistresses who give only Victorian strokes—a dozen, two dozen, perhaps fifty or even a hundred. They may state the number in advance, as with more formal punishments, or they may decide it in their heads without telling. Every stroke is a shock, however many there may be. Let the girls who say spanking is a "dolly punishment" try one of these.

Again there are those who mix Victorian strokes with ordinary hard ones. A short spanking is not so terrible, but what if it is a long one? In some ways even the cane might be preferable to a long spanking from Miss ——. At least a caning is limited. One cannot tell when this spanking will end—sometimes one fears it never will.

Then again there are the mild spankings that have one so fearful and then consist only of warming, middling-hard slaps, or which begin with ten good strokes which make one wonder how one is to endure the whole punishment and then melts gently into a light "friendly-spanking". All these whims and varieties are possible with spanking. The cane can never be so dallied with. A caning is a caning. Even the strap cannot be used lightly (in either sense of the word), but spanking is a different sort of punishment, a feminine punishment of infinite variety.

Dignity & Discipline

IT IS EVIDENT that no physical punishment can be a wholly dignified proceeding for the recipient, and there are times when it is entirely desirable to make her feel the humiliation of her position. However, the punishment as a whole: the occasion, the ritual, must have dignity, especially when inflicted by an adult. This means, of necessity, that a modicum of dignity must be allowed to the recipient. She may be shamed and subjugated; her skirts may be lifted; she may be made to feel like a very small child. All these things are acceptable and often salutary. The culprit must however be allowed to retain the dignity of a fundamentally noble, though temporarily erring, creature taking part in a venerable rite.

The aim of all discipline is to build character and to refine sensibility, not to undermine the one and abrade the other to bluntness. Punishment may sometimes humiliate but it should never degrade. If one were seeking to create a degraded child, lacking in self-respect and scarcely raising her sensibilities above the animal state, then modern discipline need play no part in one's régime. One would merely send her to a "Coca-Cola" school of thirty years ago where civilised standards were unknown, discipline lax and corporal punishment utterly forbidden. There are still such schools in the Republic of California, and any one who wishes to contemplate the true meaning of degradation should study a typical product of one or another of these institutions.

6. The Ruler

Rapping knuckles — On the back of the hand — On the open palm — On the calves — On the seat

THE RULER IS always readily to hand wherever academic work of any sort is being pursued and has long been an impromptu instrument of discipline in the hands of schoolmistresses, governesses and prefects. Its most frequent use is on the hands where it may be used in a number of ways.

Rulers vary greatly in size and weight, from light, cheap foot-rulers to heavy, eighteen-inch ebony ones. There are also yardsticks which may sometimes be used across the legs or seat, however these seem to us to have little merit as disciplinary implements, besides being liable to break in use. The most common ruler for ordinary use would be a normal foot ruler, not too light, but not extra thick nor made from one of the hardwoods. Brass-ended or brass-edged rulers should not be used for obvious reasons. Rulers of less than a foot are of little use as disciplinary implements, though we have known a mistress who could produce an exemplary sting with a nine-inch ruler held between finger and thumb.

Rapping the knuckles is a traditional punishment for inattention. The pupil extends her hand, palm down (sometimes closed or half-closed) and the flat of the ruler is brought down with a sharp crack across the first set of knuckles (i.e. those at the base of the fingers). One may also (though not with a heavy ruler) rap the more sensitive second set of knuckles. The third set should not be rapped. Raps may be hard and deliberate or delivered in rapid succession. Some mistresses favour a single hard rap for mistakes or inattention. This is particularly effective when working individually with a pupil who lacks concentration. The feeling of the mistress's close attention and the knowledge that every slip will bring her ruler down hard across one's knuckles concentrates the mind wonderfully. Music mistresses often use this method.

One may also use the ruler on the back of the hand. This is often regarded as a variant on knuckle-rapping and certainly it is an excellent way of making effective use of the lighter rulers. A hard, firm slap across the back of the hand delivers quite a sobering sting, and several of them are a not inconsiderable chastisement. The usual means of administering this punishment is to have the child hold out her hand, palm downwards. If both hands are to be punished she will hold out first one and then the other. Some mistresses, however, prefer to instruct a girl to place both hands, palm downwards, in front of her on the desk. This usually precedes a vigorous application of the ruler to both hands. Another use of this position is during recitation. A girl reciting a poem she has been set to learn, saying her irregular verbs or even answering questions on a passage from a textbook may do so with her hands on the desk, the ruler being applied for each mistake. This is particularly useful for the testing of a piece of punitive learning*. Sometimes a whole class may be told to place their hands before them on the desk during the singing of songs, chanting of tables, recitation of a poem or other piece of learning. The mistress will perambulate the aisles with her ruler, applying it to the hands of any girl who does not know the work or is not keeping time.

The other use of the ruler on the hands is on the open palm. The girl will hold out her hand palm upwards. If both hands are to be punished she will change them when instructed. It is not usual to hold out alternate hands for each stroke, as is common with the strap or the cane, although one may wish to change her hands after a number of strokes and then, when each has had an equal dose, instead of ending the punishment as she will probably expect, changing hands and giving another "round"—sometimes more than one.

The larger rulers on the open hand are very effective, and even the lighter ones give a good sting. An interesting technique was employed by one mistress of our acquaintance in the case of girls who had committed quite serious offences. She would punish them on the hands with a moderate-sized ruler and then tell

* See page 50.

them that they were to report to Miss —— at half-past five for two strokes of the cane on each hand. The psychological effect of this was considerable, for a well-employed ruler on the palm is very effective, although bearable, but the contemplation—"If a little ruler hurt that much, how shall I possibly bear the cane?" —will remain with the girl throughout the school day.

Another use of the ruler is on the calves of the legs. The lightest ruler will administer stinging chastisement to this sensitive area. This punishment is usually given to small children, but is excellent for girls of all ages, and has a healthily humiliating effect on the older girl who is rather too full of herself (for this purpose it has the great merit of hurting much more than an onlooker might suppose, often causing a great girl of sixteen to wince or gasp at her "baby punishment"). This form of correction is often used as an appropriate medicine for girls who fail to keep their stocking-seams straight.

The ruler as an instrument for punishing the seat is rather ineffective when an ordinary foot-ruler is in question. At a pinch it may administer a light sting to the unprotected thighs, but no more. A heavier eighteen- or twenty-one-inch ruler, however, can be used fairly effectively over the petticoat* or on the seat of the knickers. A wide, heavy ruler should be used, and the punishment takes the form of what might be called an over-the-desk spanking†. As an over-the-desk punishment which is deliberately rather lighter than a strapping (but may be much longer if desired) this can have its occasional uses.

* See page 97. Special schoolmistress's rulers are available in 1½-inch wide maple or poplar in lengths of twelve, eighteen and twenty-four inches. These are ideally suited to disciplinary purposes and may be used to administer a full scale spanking or even, with the twenty-four-inch variety, a formal punishment of a set number of strokes.

† See methods of spanking, page 61.

7. The Switch

Natural switch — Merits of thin switch — Transience of effect.

THAT THE SWITCH is not commonly found in the classrooms and schoolrooms of this country is, in the opinion of the present authors, one of the most regrettable omissions in our informal disciplinary system. No other implement is quite so splendidly suited to the administration of regular impromptu discipline. Switches are of various kinds. Many of those in use are simply cut-down lengths of cane, between eighteen inches and two feet in length. These can be bought from school suppliers, but are probably more often cut from light canes which have split or broken at the ends. Such switches are often kept on the mistress's desk and used for "immediate discipline" on the hands or seat. Some mistresses use the little nursery cane as a switch for older girls.

Unlike the cane, the switch need not be used to administer strokes of a uniform force, nor of a set and limited number. A brisk switching of a dozen or so strokes of medium force is entirely allowable. We know of one governess who regularly administers such a punishment to children who are dreamy or inattentive. She terms it her "wake-up punishment". A few strokes on the hand at less than full force are often ample for the needs of a particular situation, but would be impossible with a fully recognised classroom cane, for even the lesser canes have their dignity as canes. The switch, then, as a small rattan, a "little sister" to the cane, is an implement of great value and versatility.

The most traditional kind of switch, however, is one cut from a growing tree, usually birch or willow, though cherry and other trees can yield excellent switches. In Ireland the sally (willow) switch is traditionally used in schools. It is customary to send an ill-behaved child out into the grounds to cut a sally for herself.

The natural switch is very little used in modern schools, partly, perhaps, because it involves some additional effort to find and cut one rather than being always to hand as with a standard strap or cane, and perhaps even more because it has a somewhat rustic appearance which may be considered unsuited to the neat, trim atmosphere of the modern classroom (perhaps for some older mistresses it is redolent of the ghastly stripped-pine "naturalism" of the last century and all the attitudes that went with it). Actually the natural switch is a traditional implement of great charm and character, and one which deserves to be considered seriously by the neatest modern schoolmistress. A natural switch of birch or willow placed in a single-stem vase on the desk may add a whimsical touch of Art-Neo *Japonaiserie* to classroom discipline.

One of the most delightful things about a natural switch is that it can be of almost any character, from a long one as thick as a pencil, almost a minor cane, to the thinnest of switches, which administer a punishment quite unlike any other. All natural switches taper from base to tip and have a flexibility much greater than that of a piece of cane of the same length.

We particularly favour the thinner switch. Heavier switches are very effective, and can be used as an alternative to the strap, but the thin switch opens a new field of discipline. The very thinnest are birch switches which may be no thicker than a pencil-lead and up to eighteen inches in length. Such a switch looks completely harmless, but used with skill and force gives a thin, high-pitched sting which makes a girl draw in her breath. It is ideally used with the girl bending over, on her thighs, between the stocking-tops and the knickers. Two or three strokes makes a good "reminder", but it is possible to administer a severe little whipping of anything up to several dozen strokes, perhaps covering the whole area of the exposed thighs. The strokes, if well laid on, will create thin, raised welts, which quickly turn from white to red, the whole area of pale flesh rapidly reddening all over. The girl under such chastisement will tend to gasp and even wriggle. It is a fascinating punishment because its sting, though intense, is always superficial, and within a short while of its termination, both discomfort and marks have vanished; it is a curious, ætherial form of chastening which seems negligible when the switch is produced, stings fearfully, builds up to a breathtaking crescendo and then vanishes again as if it had never been.

8. The Birch

Suitability for girls — Intuitiveness of birching — The question of immodesty considered — Postures for birching Construction of a birch — Restraints.

IF THE NATURAL switch is little used in schools, her "elder sister" the birch rod is an even greater rarity both in schools and institutions and almost equally in the home. No doubt the reasons for this are similar to those which prevail in the case of the natural switch, and are redoubled, for the birch is rather more trouble to gather and prepare. Again, the birch having been a judicial implement, has gained a reputation for severity which causes it to be considered unsuitable for use on girls and young ladies in domestic or scholastic settings.

This latter impression is entirely ill-founded. The birch has been used on girls in homes and schools throughout most of our history. The birch-rods so used should not in any way be confused with the great wooden-handled judicial birches, several feet in length, with which criminal offenders have been lashed. The birch-rod as applied to girls usually varies between fourteen inches and two and a half feet in length. It may range from the small parlour-birch to the more formidable school birch, but in no case is it remotely comparable to the fearsome rods which have been used in criminal courts and in some boys' schools.

The birch has been called the most feminine instrument of discipline, and certainly its sting is quite unlike anything else, at once deeper and more intimate, gentler and more severe. "Gentler and more severe" may seem a contradiction in terms, but what we mean is this: the birch does not "strike" or cut in the way a cane or a strap does. It is yielding rather than hard, and its stroke is not so much the violent blow of one solid against another as a curious caress. Girls receiving the birch for the first time have described its impact as "watery" or like "being soaked in some soft, stinging fluid". Yet the sting itself is certainly not gentle, and a really good birching may well be more feared than the cane itself.

The birch, however, unlike the cane, is an implement of great variety. With the cane, discipline must be unvaryingly severe. A number of strokes, laid down in advance must each be given with great force. A birching is a more intuitive affair. An "average" stroke of the birch, unlike the cane, is not of maximum force, although it is certainly forceful; there may also be gentler strokes and more severe, cane-strength ones, sometimes called "Victorian" strokes. A "Victorian" birching would consist of nothing but "Victorian" strokes; perhaps a dozen or eighteen of them—a punishment in some respects more like a caning: however this is only one of the many variants of birching and not the most common one* (nor, despite the term, which is quite widely used, is there any evidence that this method was used predominantly in the reign of the first Queen Victoria). A birching may be a long punishment, like a spanking, or it may be a short, sharp one, like a switching, or, as we have seen, a short, severe one like a caning. Numbers of strokes are not normally declared in advance, so a girl preparing herself for the birch and beginning to receive her chastisement may have no idea how long she must endure it. She is entirely at her mistress's mercy: and with a birching of anything more than the mildest, she will desire that mercy most ardently. Some mistresses may declare in advance that this will be "a long birching", an announcement that fills the heart with dread, especially as the stinging strokes begin and the fiery sensation mounts.

Another reason for the current avoidance of the birch may be

---

* There has lately been a trend in some advanced schools to institute the Birch as an Ultimate Sanction. In these schools lighter canes are not used and the full School Cane is employed as an intermediate discipline, so that "getting the Cane", while still not commonplace, is a sanction fairly freely applied by mistresses: either personally or, more usually, by sending girls for a formal caning. But for very serious offences—and only for those—the Birch is invoked.

In these schools, birching is always "Victorian", with so many strokes formally applied at full strength; sentences normally ranging from twelve to three dozen.

the idea that it cannot be applied without immodesty. It is certainly true that the birch can only be satisfactorily applied to the unclothed skin. Some matrons and housemistresses using the birch require a girl to appear wearing a dressing-gown put on back-to-front with no clothing beneath it. She will then be lain face-down on a bed or couch and the dressing-gown untied and opened for the laying on of the strokes. This, of course is rather at variance with modern standards of modesty, and in most schools would be in direct contravention of modesty regulations. However, this degree of disrobing is far from necessary for girls, although for the other sex a degree of immodesty which is generally unacceptable is impossible to avoid, and it is perhaps this fact that has discouraged its use in schools in general.

The most usual method of applying the birch in girls' schools is to use a birching-table. This may be any table which will permit a girl to bend over it, lying her upper body flat along its surface. The skirt and petticoats are then lifted up and the birch applied to her upper thighs. For most punishments the area between the knickers and the tops of the stockings is entirely adequate, though when a severer punishment or a larger birch is being used it is sometimes necessary to unfasten the suspenders and lower the stockings to the knees—not because one would strike so low, but to ensure that the delicate film of the stockings is not caught and laddered by stray twigs.

To those who will argue that this method is entirely unsatisfactory and that no true birching can be given without further disrobing, we can only say that we have seen it in regular use both in schools and by private governesses, and that it is highly effective and has stood the test of time and wide usage. Many girls who have grown up to fear the birch above all other chastisements—and we must include one of the authoresses of the present treatise among their number—have known it applied in no other way.

With the same degree of exposure the birch may also be used over a school desk or lying face down on a bed. These "lying-down" birchings are often the severest, the girl being placed in a comfortable position to receive long and hard chastisement. It is sometimes considered advisable to place a pillow or even two underneath the girl in the correct position to raise her seat higher than the rest of her body and set her thighs at the correct angle as well as stretching the skin to a more punishable firmness.

The birch-rod itself may vary from a long, slender bundle of a few birch switches to a wide, bushy implement in which each individual rod has many ramifying twigs. These twigs should be thin and slender and as supple as possible. Each style of birch has its own special qualities and different mistresses prefer different sorts, the wisest, in our view, being those who are familiar with various types and seek, with each girl upon each separate occasion, to choose both the rod and the mode of birching that her inner self requires.

Birching can have great deal in common with spanking in that it can be a long and highly intuitive communion with the girl being disciplined. Birchings of this nature should be rhythmic and may pass through many phases; from slow, heavy strokes to fast, vigorous ones, to gentle ones which keep the rhythm while letting the child relax and recover herself. A birching of this sort is best given in a lying position and it may be advisable to fasten the girl by attaching her wrists and ankles to the head and foot of the bed (this is most possible with the iron-framed beds commonly found in schools and institutions). Such fastening is for the purpose not only of preventing rebellion (which is not often necessary) but also of giving the child a greater sense of security and "enclosure" which is a vital part of such a punishment, for the "caressing" nature of the birch comes very much into its own here, and while such punishments are indeed very painful, they are also acts of warmth and love, and are felt as such by all but the coldest and most insensitive child.

9. The Strap

Difference from the Tawse — Types of strap — Number of strokes to be given — Suitable strapping positions Punishments on the hand — Compound punishments Culprits' permitted reactions

THE STRAP HAS latterly become a familiar part of English school life. In Scotland it has always been used, and in that country is commonly known as the tawse—an instrument made of a heavy grade of leather and, in the case of the sturdier examples, every bit as formidable as the cane itself. This is as it should be, since in Scotland the cane is rarely used, and many schools do not possess one at all, a tawse of greater length and weight, usually three-tailed, taking its place as the ultimate deterrent.

The English school strap is usually a rather less fearsome thing than the tawse, and although it has been in use for a considerable time (19th century examples may often be seen in museums and other collections and sometimes come up for sale in antique shops), it seems to have come into its own in the present century. While the Scottish implement is long, often quite narrow and heavy, the English strap is generally shorter, broader and lighter (that is to say, the leather is not so thick). We say generally, because English straps come in a wide variety of types and designs, some resembling the tawse in appearance, but very rarely of the same weight. This will be understood when we explain that the leather of a tawse is normally some four-sixteenths of an inch thick—that is, as thick as a Junior school cane—and of a very hard, dense grade of hide. Its effect is that of a heavy, penetrating sting, somewhere between a slap and a blow, and if used with great force will leave discolouration which may last for some days.

The English strap, on the other hand, has a lighter sting, although still a very considerable one. It comes, as we have said, in different forms, the most common being sixteen to eighteen inches long and three to three-and-a-half inches broad with one end shaped as a "handle" and the other divided into two tails. It may be used on the hands or on the seat. It is not usually used over the skirt, but the heavier versions may sometimes be so. Normally it is used over the petticoat. It may also be applied to the seat of the knickers. Other variants include the "looped" or doubled strap, a typical example being eighteen inches long by eleven inches wide, the thong, which is two-sixteenths of an inch thick, leaving the six-inch solid handle (which is included in the overall length) and forming a great loop which returns to the handle again, the strap thus being a double thickness of leather. In theory this may sound almost as formidable as a tawse, but it is not. Its effect is that of a spreading, tingling slap, very intense at first, but of no real depth, and quickly diminishing. This may be applied to the same areas as other straps, though an ardent advocate of its use tells us that she considers it most effective when applied to the unprotected upper thigh just below the protection of the knickers and above the level of the stockings. On unclothed skin, the tingling sting reaches its greatest intensity, particularly when several strokes are applied at a brisk, though unhurried, pace.

There are also light straps designed for frequent "minor-corrective" use, canvas-backed rubber straps which are said to produce a ferocious sting, especially on the hands, while leaving no after-effects (these are rare in this country, but traditional in the Dominion of Canada), heavy, three-tailed straps for serious punishments, and many other types. Light, limp straps with plaited handles are sometimes employed and many more members of the strap family are available for different occasions and tastes.

The strap in the English school is very much a classroom instrument. It often lies on the mistress's desk in view of the class, or is kept in the desk to be brought out either when it is to be used or as a warning that it may be used soon. It is essentially an alternative to the classroom cane, and in many schools today it replaces the classroom cane altogether, either because it is considered a less formidable instrument for daily use or because it is considered important to keep the cane "special", the only cane in the school being a full-sized one used only on serious occasions. Even though there is little confusion between classroom canes and the Cane itself, we are of the opinion that there is a great deal of psychological wisdom in this approach.

The strap, however, should not be underrated as a disciplinary implement. It is true that only the tawse is equivalent to a full-sized school cane, but a good English strap may well mete out a punishment equal to (though different in quality from) that delivered by one of the lighter classroom canes. Indeed, the more matter-of-fact attitude often taken by mistresses toward the administration of the strap may give it an effectiveness of quite another sort from that of the cane. Resting in full view on a hook or on the mistress's desk, the strap may often be freely applied for classroom misdemeanours, its dark, polished-leather presence adding a sombre note to the scholastic atmosphere and its unrelenting sting perhaps all the more startling because one is not ritually and psychologically prepared for it to the same degree, as is the case with a caning.

"A dose of the strap" is an excellent cure for inattention, talking in class, untidy uniform and similar faults, while a more serious strapping can be applied for most offences up to those which require the school cane.

In addition to the classroom strap, many schools have a more formidable strap, often kept by a senior mistress or one who is temperamentally suited to the exercise of formal disciplinary duties, which is used for more serious offences. In schools where a caning is a rarity, this may represent a half-way (or three-quarter-way) stage between everyday chastisement and the ultimate sanction of the cane. These straps are much feared, and go by various names, such as the House Strap, the School Strap, a Formal Strapping, or just "a strapping from Miss ——". Often the mistress and the strap are closely associated, and the instruction "You will report to Miss Smith for fifteen strokes of the strap" has a dread effect of quite another order from an ordinary command to bend over the desk for a strapping.

The number of strokes given with the English strap differs somewhat from numbers given with the cane. Numbers under four are unusual, and many mistresses and prefects, when using a strap that is not too heavy will award strokes in dozens, normally one, two or three dozen. The classroom strap, however, is usually a rather harder, heavier implement with which six to a dozen is an effective punishment (necessarily so, as one would not wish to disrupt a lesson by administering a lengthy strapping). With the cane it is customary always to declare in advance the number of strokes to be given; in the case of a spanking with a hairbrush, slipper or other implement such a declaration is rare, the punishment being more "intuitive" and less "judicial". The strap may be used in either way. One may either give a set number of hard strokes, as with the cane (and in the classroom this is most usual), or administer a "good strapping" which proceeds until the administratrix decides that the punishment is complete.

In the dormitory and the home, the strap is often applied in a lying position. The girl is instructed to lie face down upon her bed, her skirts are raised and the strap applied to her seat and upper thighs. Usually this position is adopted for a long strapping of several dozen strokes, usually with a longish strap or even a leather belt (although the latter is rarely used in schools). The nature of this punishment may described as "severe but homely". The position adopted is easy to maintain (although for very severe discipline a child may need to be held or secured) and comfortable, the surroundings are informal (or, in the case of a dormitory, semi-formal), but at the same time the act of lying down implies a "settling in" for a serious chastisement. This mode of punishment is traditionally given to maidservants who have transgressed badly and require a good whipping to cancel out their fall from grace and re-establish them in the household. This is a fact well known to most young ladies and one which adds an extra piquancy to the occasion. Such punishments are often delivered with a long strap or belt and may either consist of a high, declared number of strokes, or be given "feelingly" over a period. These "feeling" punishments may alternate periods of severe beating, with gentler intervals of rhythmic, almost caressing strokes. The index of the punishment may be the redness of the girl's legs, and in some punishments the aim may be to produce a uniform lividness from the back of the knees to the top of the thighs.

Such punishments are not really "school" punishments, but certain mistresses favour them in some cases, and a senior may sometimes use them upon a girl with whom she has a profound disciplinary *rapport*. They are, for the right girl at the right time, warm, important, heart-opening punishments, punishments which bind and caress and heal (hence, no doubt, their use for maidservants—always for trusted maidservants who are "part of the family", never for mere "hired girls"). Punishments like this should not be used lightly, but they should be borne in mind as a very special part of the disciplinary repertoire.

"Lying down" strappings can also be given in a lighter form as salutary dormitory or bedtime punishments. We know of a matron who, when a dormitory is noisy or restless will make all the girls lie face down on their beds and proceed from one to the other administering a dozen strokes apiece, sometimes with the occasional six for a quiet girl or two dozen for a ringleader.

Punishments on the Hands

USING THE STRAP on the hand is much easier than caning the hands. The strap is shorter and much less dangerous to use. If you do catch the wrist or thumb it will do no real harm, although, of course, one should practise until such accidents do not occur. The most common procedure for punishing on the hands is as follows:

The pupil should stand upright before the mistress with her hands by her sides or behind her. On the command; "Hold out your right hand", she will extend it before her at elbow height, opened flat with the thumb kept well down. Usually strokes are delivered on alternate hands, so a resounding stroke is laid across the right hand, a few seconds are allowed for the sting to permeate, then the command is given, "Right hand down, left hand out."

Some mistresses prefer one hand to be placed upon the other for extra support, and this is particularly recommended if the girl is very frightened and has a tendency to pull her hand away.

Strokes of the strap can be delivered cross-wise along the palm taking care to avoid the thumb, or, alternatively, the mistress can stand directly in front of the girl and deliver the stroke lengthways along the fingers and palm. The heaviest part of the stroke falls on the palm and not the fingers though it is advisable to ensure that the girl's cuff is pulled down to protect the wrist from the end of the strap should the stroke fall slightly incorrectly. It is our opinion that the hand is better held lengthways as it presents a larger target and there is less chance of catching the thumb.

The traditional Scottish method for delivering the strokes cannot be bettered. The mistress stands in position, that is, either to the side for a cross-palm stroke, or directly in front of the pupil and lets the strap fall behind her shoulder and down her back. Her hand rests lightly upon her shoulder with her forearm and elbow against her chest. At the commencement of the stroke she brings her hand sharply down moving only her forearm and keeping her elbow against her body. The strap describes an arc in the air, its weight and the swift movement of the mistress's arm ensuring that it lands with a resounding crack. With a little practice great accuracy can be produced as the strap itself does the work. It is important to stand well away from the pupil allowing plenty of room for the length of the strap and the length of the forearm.

Punishment on the hand is in many ways more difficult for the pupil to accept than that on the seat. She is unsupported and must keep her hand still by her own efforts. Even an unsupported bending-over position is much easier to maintain—it may be difficult, but the only alternatives are standing up and collapsing, both of which are too drastic to be seriously considerable. Withdrawing the hand, though, is simple, natural and almost instinctive. Some girls will try to withdraw the hand before the stroke connects. This must be regarded as a very serious offence, however frightened the girl may be. She must be warned about it in advance if she looks nervous or likely to withdraw. It is an understandable fault, but it would be disastrous for discipline if it was not corrected with considerable severity—particularly if it takes place in public as a majority of hand-strappings do. The usual punishment for withdrawing before the stroke is a serious strapping over the desk, or even a caning, followed by the original punishment, this time (usually) taken properly. Another method, less common, but perhaps even more effective in cases where a child is bad at accepting punishment, is the use of a long imposition. This should not be less than five hundred lines and may be up to a thousand. It should be stated in advance of the strapping. It has great psychological value, for the difference in duration between the two punishments is brought very forcibly to the girl's mind: "If I cannot keep my hand still for a few minutes now, I shall be writing lines for hours—and then I shall have to hold my hand out at the end of it all."

The thought of this is usually sufficient, but occasionally the imposition has to be given. It should be given in this way: "Very well, Susan, you will sit in that desk at the back of the class and write six hundred times 'I must accept punishment meekly and submissively.' When you have finished we shall try the strap again and see if you desire a further six hundred." This is, in our experience, always effective. The girl who has withdrawn her hand at eleven o'clock in the morning and who finishes her imposition at three o'clock in the afternoon will very rarely prolong the imposition into the evening hours by withdrawing her hand again. She has had a long, tedious time to consider the folly and pointlessness of her brief rebellion (for rebellion it is, however much nervousness may be present) and the inevitability of submission.

Alternatively, the lines may be set in the more usual way, the girl being ordered to present them tomorrow or the next day (depending upon the length of the imposition) when the strap will be tried again. Again, a long detention may be ordered: the lines will be written under supervision, the strapping taking place at the end.

This method, as we have said, is psychologically effective and also has the virtue of avoiding the piling-up of physical chastisement in the case of a girl who, while she must learn to "take her medicine" when necessary, may be genuinely physically sensitive. Of course, in some cases, where the element of rebellion is judged to be high, further corporal discipline may be just what the girl needs (and probably unconsciously wants). Needless to say there is nothing to prevent one from issuing both the imposition and a physical punishment. Either the whipping may be given first as an immediate retribution for rebellion followed by the long, tedious imposition and finally another chance to hold one's hand out, or the imposition may come first, being written in the knowledge that it is to be followed by a sound caning or a good dose of the heavy strap, and finally the punishment which would have been all one had to suffer if only one had accepted it in the first place.

Withdrawing one's hand *after* the stroke has landed is a much more venial offence. There is no attempt to frustrate the lawful punishment, only a natural reflex to take one's hand away from the pain, clasp it to the breast, tuck it under the arm, or merely bring it into one's protective "aura". Attitudes vary as to what should be done about this. Some mistresses, provided it is done without unnecessary "fuss" and the hand is replaced quickly (not because the same hand is usually punished immediately—although it sometimes is—but because the order to hold out the hand has not yet been rescinded) allow this natural reflex to pass unreprimanded. Others hold that the instinct can be commanded (as indeed it can) and should. An order to extend the hand remains in force until rescinded and any withdrawal is an offence. Some declare a stroke null and void if the hand is withdrawn after it, and give it again. Others will award lines—say fifty—for each stroke rendered unsatisfactory by a failure to maintain the hand submissively in position. The authors tend towards this latter position, which, while it may seem severe at first, is not excessively so. Girls quickly learn to keep the hand in place and avoid the extra penalties. A good, disciplined acceptance of punishment is much neater and more pleasing than unseemly displays of flinching.

The problem of grimacing is one that occurs only with punishments given on the hand, partly because the face is not visible during other forms of corporal chastisement, but also because they do not provide the same inducement to contort the features. This, in itself, is an interesting reflection of the different *tone* of punishments given on the hand. A punishment on the seat may well be more severe, but it does not cause the same wincing sensation as a less severe one given on the hands. These punishments bring forth the natural rebellion and withdrawal of a child on a *somatic* level where it may be dealt with. This is why the forbidding of flinchings and withdrawals, even after the event, is important. One is training the child to conquer her instinctive rebellion and submit herself fully. The question of grimacing may be tackled in a slightly different way. It is unsightly and undignified and must be corrected—indeed, this is an important lesson in keeping one's dignity and lady-like poise even under difficult circumstances, and therefore a vitally important one to learn. However many girls find it all but impossible not to give some evidence of the wince which they experience. While some mistresses simply insist that it be suppressed as far as humanly possible, another method is to permit, and even encourage, a degree of crying aloud. This crying, must, of course, be delicate, maidenly, and, with girls of a better class, accord with the principles of elocution which they have been taught (a nice, round, well-formed "Oh!"). Of the two methods we prefer this latter—although crying aloud should only be permitted in the case of severer punishments. A few strokes of a light strap should be taken in silence and with a composed demeanour.

10. The Cane

An unparalleled token of disapproval — Where it may be encountered — Its mystique — Legal status Dimensions & Weights: Junior, Senior, Disciplinary & Nursery Canes defined —The Office Cane Grades of rattan — Similarity of qualities to those of fine wines —The "lesser" canes administered by senior schoolgirls — Domestic canings — Caning technique Canings "to order" by qualified Third Parties—Using the cane — Psychological preparation — Postures for caning — Preparation of clothing — Caning on the hands — Number of strokes — Care of the cane.

THE CANE IS the archetypal implement of English school discipline. Stroke for stroke, a good quality standard school cane probably administers the most intense sting of any instrument of correction and is greatly feared by schoolchildren everywhere. To be put down for the cane (meaning the School Cane rather than any lesser implement) is the most signal mark of official disapprobation. In Supported schools and other public institutions, this punishment must be entered in the Punishment Book as a permanent record of the gravity of the offence and the seriousness of the chastisement, and most private schools, colleges *&cetera* keep a similar Punishment Book. Parents or guardians must be informed of a caning administered to their charges, and will doubtless express their displeasure at the necessity for such chastisement, not infrequently imposing further punishment of their own. A caning is thus both an intensely painful event and a public disgrace of no minor gravity.

The cane is today increasingly employed in the home and in some offices as well as in ladies' University colleges and other institutions concerned with the education and training of young women. The use of the cane in the home is not so much an innovation as a return to a tradition which was disrupted in the 20th century by the notoriously unhealthy attitudes toward discipline which prevailed, particularly in the latter part of the century.

The cane may be used either on the hands or on the hinder parts. The latter is both more usual and safer. Attitudes to the employment of the cane vary, but it is generally considered that it is not an implement which should be used too frequently. It has a certain "mystique" as something approaching an Ultimate Sanction and the announcement that a girl is to receive the cane should produce a sense of awe both in the girl herself and in her classmates or companions. The occasion of standing outside a mistress's study, or remaining in class after lessons are over, awaiting a caning, is one of the most frightening in a girl's scholastic career. It should not be allowed to become dulled by over-frequency, and when a caning is decided upon, it should never be allowed to be an anti-climax.

With the cane every stroke must be clean, very hard and painfully effective. A caning is not a gentle or homely punishment. It is one of the most serious forms of discipline and should be treated as such. If one is inclined to shew mercy, this must be considered before a caning is ordained and will take the form either of a smaller number of strokes or of dispensing with the cane altogether in favour of a strapping, a spanking or some other punishment in which lenity may more legitimately be exercised: but every stroke of the cane should be a stroke to remember. The mistress who, from a mistaken sense of kindness, should fail in this particular is letting down her very function as a mistress. The cane is a serious punishment and must be used seriously or not at all.

The Cane and the Law

THE NORMAL ENGLISH cane is a straight, flexible rattan rod with a crook handle. It may vary considerably in weight, length and thickness, and certain specifications are laid down by the Home Office for use in Supported schools, Government orphan asylums and other public places. It should be noted that these regulations do not apply to private schools which may use more formidable implements if they choose, though in our view, and in that of a majority of headmistresses, the official guidelines provide a sensible and accepted standard for normal school purposes.

The standard Junior cane, then, is twenty-eight inches in length and four-sixteenths of an inch in thickness. This is authorised for use on children between eight and twelve. The standard Senior cane is thirty-three inches in length and five-sixteenths of an inch in thickness and is authorised for use on children between thirteen and twenty-one. Girls over twenty-one in full time education in public institutions such as the Universities, colleges and training hospitals may be caned at the discretion of the institutional authorities or their immediate superiors if so authorised by those authorities, using a cane of the specification of the senior school cane.

These specifications designate "upper limits", and smaller implements may freely be employed where this is considered desirable. There is also a category of cane known as the Disciplinary cane which may be employed on girls eligible for the senior school cane in cases where extreme disciplinary measures are considered necessary. The Disciplinary cane is thirty-six inches in length and six-sixteenths of an inch in thickness and may only be administered by, on the instruction of, or with the express permission of, a headmistress, college principal or equivalent. Under similar circumstances, the Senior school cane may be employed on girls under thirteen.

For children under eight a Nursery cane is authorised for use in Supported schools and other public institutions undertaking the care of young children. This cane is twenty-one inches long and three-sixteenths of an inch in thickness—a very short, light implement which is often used with the child over the knee (a thing quite impossible with even the shortest of normal school canes). Occasionally such canes are used for other than nursery purposes. In some schools they are issued to monitors or prefects, and with practice one may learn to deliver a waspish sting to an older girl in the normal bending position by using the cane as forcibly as if it were a "real" one. Obviously, such an implement is entirely ineffective applied over even a tight skirt, and is always used over—or under—the petticoat. Some mistresses keep them for use in classes of older girls as a switch for the hands, and some firms supply a longer cane in this very thin nursery grade. This is

Standard Home Office length & diameter specifications for punishment canes (female)

Nursery Cane 21" x $\frac{3}{16}$"

Junior (and Office) Cane 30" (32") x $\frac{4}{16}$"

Senior Cane 33" x $\frac{5}{16}$"

Disciplinary Cane 36" x $\frac{6}{16}$"

Actual Size

a curious implement which delivers a punishment, hardly to be termed a caning at all in the normal understanding of the term, but very effective as a sharp punishment of moderate severity in its own right.

In offices and places of employment, the Home Office authorises the use of an office cane which may be thirty inches in length and four-sixteenths of an inch in thickness. The office cane may be used only in cases where such use is clearly stipulated in the Terms of Employment agreed to by the employee. There has been some criticism of the fact that the largest cane which may be used on grown office-girls (usually over their skirts) is only a little more formidable than the junior school cane and considerably less so than the senior school cane. However the sting of such an implement should not be underestimated (and is not by any who has felt it), and is generally subjectively greater when experienced by girls unused to corporal punishment. It should also be borne in mind that the element of shame and humiliation entailed in the punishment of an independent working girl is considerably greater than that felt by a schoolgirl: and this is so even when comparing an office-girl of fifteen and a uniformed sixth-former of eighteen.

Types of Cane

WE HAVE ALREADY discussed the major categories of cane recognised by the Law. These are the canes most generally used in homes and institutions, and the expression "getting the cane" would normally refer to receiving a stated number of strokes from that one of the implements discussed above applicable to one's age and station.

Nevertheless there are various other considerations to be taken into account in a discussion of types of cane. To begin with, the bare legal definition of length and thickness does not tell us all we need to know about an individual cane, for there are well over a hundred different types of rattan, a score or more of which are suitable for disciplinary purposes. The "average" cane is light in colour and of what we may term a middling weight, but there are darker, denser grades of rattan which produce an implement which both looks and feels considerably more formidable. (In the last century this became very difficult to obtain, but it is now being grown and imported commercially once more). These are often chosen by governesses and schoolmistresses who wish to make a pronounced impression on their charges and ensure that the cane is held in proper awe. It is thus that certain canes—"the housemistress's cane" for example, may gain a reputation for being "a real scorcher" even though it conforms to precisely the same legal definition as the other canes in the school. In a number of schools we have known canes of this type to be referred to as "Victorian canes" (referring, of course, to the reign of Queen Victoria the First), and indeed, we feel that the term has a certain aptness and charm. One of the writers recalls from her own childhood a particular cane employed on rare occasions by her governess. It was a straight-handled cane, the handle being a leather-bound grip, and it was if anything a little shorter and thinner than her usual crook-handled implement, but it was of a dark, dense-looking rattan, and a caning with this was really an experience to be dreaded.

Another important variation in the "quality" of canes is that of flexibility. Three canes of precisely the same length and thickness may vary remarkably in flexibility. One may be so flexible that it may be bent with a light grip into a three-quarter circle. In use it will arc into a semi-circle and whip back sharply. It takes considerable skill to control and place it. Used correctly, though, like swimming or riding a bicycle, it is one of those skills which, however daunting it may appear at first, is mastered relatively quickly and then retained. There is no excuse for a fully-trained schoolmistress to be incapable of using the longest and whippiest of canes. The second cane of our hypothetical threesome may be really quite stiff. Of course, it will not be stiff like bamboo (a cane which inexperienced people sometimes try to use for disciplinary purposes—it should never be so used), it will bend when flexed in the hand and curve when swished through the air, but relatively little. The third cane is of a standard flexibility. It bends easily into a quarter-circle and can be forced into, or nearly into, a semi-circle without distortion of its straightness when it springs back. Obviously these are only three points on a scale that includes many subtle gradations. The degree of flexibility is not directly related to the weight or density of the rattan: one may have a light stiff cane or a light whippy one, a heavy stiff cane or a heavy whippy one—so one may see that taking these two considerations together, a cane of exactly thirty three inches in length and five-sixteenths of an inch in thickness (and thickness is rarely exact) may in fact possess an infinite variety of characteristics, making an individual cane almost as particular as an individual mistress. We should note, though, that the "Victorian" grade of cane rarely if ever comes into the very flexible category.

The choice of the degree of flexibility of a cane is very much a matter of sensibility. One does not necessarily punish more effectively than another, but it punishes with a different *tone.* The firm, thwacking bite of the stiffest cane and the shrill sting of the whippiest may be equal in the degree of punishment they inflict, but it is a very different *kind* of punishment, and between these two lie many fine shades. Some mistresses use only the most flexible canes and choose them as long and whippy as they may; others prefer the straightness and starched severity of a good firm rod, and many take what we hold to be the best course, that of choosing upon each occasion, from a number of canes, that which seems most to suit the girl and the moment. More than one mistress of my acquaintance actually has names for her canes. One is called Marianna, a slender, swishing willowy young lady, delicate but strict with the passion and fierce purity of supple youth, another is Agnes, an older and severely unbending dame, meting out her undeviating measure of sound correction. This may seem fanciful to some, but in our view it is an excellent means of attuning one's mind to the inner quality of each cane and the punishment she makes possible, and considering it in the light of the girl to be disciplined, her offence, her state of mind and the inward needs of her young heart. For punishment, let it never be forgotten, however little it may be desired, is the fulfillment of an inward need, the righting of a balance, the bringing of a child to herself again; and the more sensitive, the more finely-tuned, this punishment may be, the better will it serve this subtlest but most important of its purposes.

In addition to these qualitative differences, there are many canes which are measurably different from the standard combinations of length and thickness laid down by Law for different purposes. Some of these are larger or more severe than the legal categories, but as these are not permitted in Supported schools and other public institutions (though they may, of course, be used in private schools and homes) we shall not discuss them here. There are, however, various lighter-than-normal canes. These may be freely used in Supported schools and elsewhere and are often employed for a variety of purposes. One well-known supplier, for example, has two canes known as the Prefect and the Monitress. The Prefect is twenty-six inches long and four-sixteenths of an inch thick: the Monitress is twenty-four inches long and five-sixteenths of an inch thick. The Monitress is made of specially lightweight rattan and is described as "a light, stiffish cane with a flat, slapping bite", while the Prefect is described as "a shortish but flexible cane with a thin, sharp sting". Note that there comes a point when the appreciation of canes is not dissimilar to that of wines or fine brandies, and the precise *nuances* of their sting must be described in terms which hint, within the limitations of language, at their subtle qualities, for the language of physical sensation, like that of taste, is woefully undeveloped in comparison to that of visual and mental phenomena: so just as a single-malt whisky may be described as "smoky", "earthy" or "fruity", so the sting of a cane may be described as "strap-like",(although of course, no cane is really anything like a strap), "sharp but firm" or "shrill". One should also bear in mind that these catalogue descriptions can only be of a fairly general application. Every cane, being a natural rather than an artificial thing, has its own precise qualities and is not exactly like any other cane. Of course, many canes of the same type and specification are broadly similar, but some canes have great individuality and special qualities and many a mistress will have one particular cane which she cherishes and knows can never be exactly replaced.

To return, however, to the smaller and lighter canes exemplified by the Prefect and the Monitress cited above: such canes, clearly, do not have the same force and mystique as the more standard school and institutional canes, but they do have various important uses. The first is implied in the names of the examples given: these lighter implements are not infrequently issued to a Head Girl for use by school prefects, often a more formidable one for senior prefects and a less formidable one for junior prefects or monitresses, but neither as formidable as the canes employed by the mistresses. In strict private households the use of such lighter canes is sometimes allowed to an elder sister or cousin, and we have heard of such implements being made available to upper maidservants for use on their subordinates or even on the children of the house.

"Lesser" canes may also be used in schools by the mistresses, and we have often encountered such institutions as "the classroom cane", "the detention cane" and "the dormitory cane". Each of these would normally be a lighter instrument than a standard school cane, though each would have its own characteristics and would be used more frequently than the standard implement. The classroom cane, which hangs in view of the class or is kept in a classroom cupboard and brought out for infractions of classroom discipline, may be used whenever the mistress deems it necessary. Some advanced mistresses may normally expect to use it once or twice in the course of a lesson. The detention cane, rather severer than the classroom cane, is used in the longer and more serious detentions, wherein each small infraction merits the strap or rod. The dormitory cane is a lighter implement, used over the nightdress and considered ideal, with its sharp, sobering sting, for quelling bedtime fractiousness.

None of these canes really merits the patrician title of "the cane", and they are by no means dreaded in the same way. They are often made straight, without the customary crook handle, to make the distinction clearer. Their special names should be used clearly and regularly, so that the solemn institution of the Cane itself should not fall into familiar contempt. Only prefects and monitresses refer to the use of these canes as *getting the cane* with the full weighty overtone of that expression, and it is well understood that "getting the cane" from a girl is not at all the same thing as getting it from a mistress, although, of course, most schoolgirls, given caning authority, will do their best to put a ferocious sting into their youthful chastisements; and any girl who has been on the receiving end of such attentions will confirm that they often do very well indeed.

These smaller canes are ideal for use on the hands, and are also often used as blackboard pointers. Indeed, many mistresses do not refer to them as canes at all, but regard them as pointers which have a secondary disciplinary purpose. This notion maintains even more firmly their differentiation from the Cane itself: a whipping with the pointer being considered an entirely different species of punishment from a true caning.

Many mothers choose one of these lighter instruments for a household cane, and this, or the fact that mothers are often untrained in the art of caning, may often render a "home caning" a rather less daunting event than a school caning. Perhaps this is inevitable, and many mothers would not wish it otherwise, though for our part we would advocate the retention of at least one "serious" cane in the home and would recommend that mothers and others in charge of children should take some instruction in the art of caning. Many schools offer lessons in this at a very modest fee, and a single lesson will enable most ladies to administer a sensible, effective caning. The more serious cane may never be used, but its existence and the knowledge that it can be used to proper effect has a greatly beneficial influence upon the standing of the mistress of the house.

It is increasingly understood in these days that the Archetype of the mother is of incalculable psychological value to children. We now know that a whole generation has been irreparably damaged by the casual, deracinated overgrown-teenager mothers of the late 20th century, and every enlightened modern mother attempts, in dignity, in femininity and in kindness to portray her own unique refraction of the true Archetype to the best of her ability. Authority is an important part of this Archetype, and while the use of the cane is certainly not appropriate for all, it should be more widely considered than is yet the case. It should also be borne in mind that where a mother does not wish to cane her children herself, many local training colleges these days will make available a trainee governess or schoolmistress at a very moderate fee to administer a caning at the college or sometimes in the home. Indeed, since "live" caning practice is so beneficial, and indeed vital, to the trainee governess or mistress, this service is sometimes made available gratis. Thus the warning, "If this occurs again, Deborah, you will be soundly caned" may be issued effectively even by the mother who prefers not to administer the cane herself.

USING THE CANE

Caning is an accomplishment which must be learned. Some people have a natural aptitude for it, others find it difficult, but every one who wishes to employ the cane as a means of discipline should learn the rudiments of its use. The best way to learn is to be instructed by some one who is used to caning girls: however we shall make bold to offer some general advice.

Psychological Preparation

A CANING, as we have already stated, is a serious punishment, and its seriousness should be impressed upon the girl to be disciplined by a period of psychological preparation. This may take various forms, but under no circumstances should the cane be administered in a casual, matter-of-fact manner (we are speaking here, of course, of a true caning rather than the "minor" canings administered with such instruments as the classroom cane—though even these should be performed with a certain degree of ritual). Usually there should be a period of waiting for the punishment, during which its importance may be appreciated and a feeling of anticipation may develop. In some schools canings are only administered on a particular day, so that a girl put down for a caning must wait until, say, Saturday afternoon for the execution of the sentence. Often canings are only given by particular mistresses, either in view of their senior status or because they are the most proficient in the effective use of the rod. In such cases, a formal printed slip may be made out by the mistress ordaining the punishment which must be taken by the pupil to the mistress who is to administer the discipline and countersign the slip. A stern interview will follow, after which the girl may be caned there and then, or may be given an appointment for a caning at some later time, according to established procedure or the decision of the mistress, as the case may be.

These periods of preparation are what one might call "long-term preparation", lasting some hours or even days. They are not always employed, but are well worth considering. Do ensure, however, that a caning thus prepared for is a very effective one when it finally comes, else the final effect upon the pupil may be the very reverse of that intended: a sense of "well, that was a lot of fuss over nothing much after all".

More immediate periods of preparation are also important. The traditional method of making a pupil wait outside the study of the mistress administering the chastisement is a time-honoured and sensible procedure. Where more than one girl is being caned (as occurs with group offences or when canings are carried out on a particular day of the week) girls may be made to queue outside the room in silence, perhaps hearing the sounds of their classmates' chastisement and seeing them emerge flushed and tearful. In such cases it is considered best to range girls in order of the number of strokes they are to receive, with the girl with the mildest punishment going in first and the girl with the most serious punishment waiting until last.

Many mistresses consider it rather hurried to proceed directly to a serious caning and prefer to give a girl other punitive tasks in preparation—perhaps an hour or two writing lines with the cane placed upon the mistress's desk in readiness, or out of sight but very much in mind. The writing of a letter requesting the punishment is another favoured device, sometimes following the completion of the preparatory lines. In this the girl must ask for the caning she is to receive, and in some cases must request earnestly that it be hard and painful and that her tears be not regarded. In this connexion, it should be noted that many mistresses are firmly of the opinion that a serious caning should never be unaccompanied by a lengthy written imposition either before or afterwards or, often, both. The theory is that a caning is too serious a punishment to be allowed to be "over" too quickly, and we know numerous mistresses who never fail to set several hundred lines to be written after the corporal part of the punishment is over, often with the warning that further strokes of the cane may be expected if the lines are less than perfectly executed. Such mistresses believe it to be important that a girl go forth from a caning not with a sense of light-hearted relief, but with one of heaviness and continued regret for her misdeeds.

In our view, in this as in other cases, each punishment should be weighed on its individual character. The caning which is terrible and then over is one sort of punishment. That which is preceded by a period of detention and comes to a painful climax is another. That which, when the worst seems to be over, tails off into a lengthy and tedious imposition is another again. All have their merits and should be considered for particular girls and particular misdemeanours. In our view, there are definitely times when the punishment should be over when the caning is complete—times when it is important for the girl to feel that she has paid the price and emerged fresh, clean and purified from the place of chastisement; equally, on other occasions the punishment should seem weighty and all but interminable. Some mistresses favour imposition before and after a caning—say a hundred lines while sitting in anticipation and three hundred afterwards. The latter may be set to be written in the girl's spare time, or she may be presented with the discovery that she is not to leave the place of punishment until the lengthy task has been completed, perhaps never knowing for certain whether she has really seen and felt the last of the rod. We know of more than one school where it is a general rule to impose fifty lines per stroke of the cane.

The most immediate psychological preparation of all comes in the final minutes before the caning. Perhaps a lecture will be given, perhaps not. The technique of flexing the cane may sound rather hackneyed but it is highly recommended. It is sensible for the mistress to get the "feel" of the implement and to make a demonstration of its characteristic flexibility and "spring" to the girl awaiting its kiss. More subtly, it conveys to the girl a sense of the mistress's good will toward the punishment: her resolution to carry it out effectively, her personal *rapport* with the instrument of correction, and indeed her manifestation of the Archetype of the disciplining Mistress.

Postures for Caning

THERE IS THEN the physical preparation of the girl for her punishment. This consists of placing her in position—normally bending over a desk or chair. Some mistresses favour the unsupported posture, touching the toes or holding the ankles. This is said to result in a somewhat more painful punishment; however we do not generally advocate this posture for serious canings. For the classroom or dormitory cane, and for lighter home canings, it is entirely satisfactory, but for the ordeal of a "real" caning, it is both humane and sensible to allow the child some support. The problem of "jumping up" is much greater with unsupported punishments, and although some prefects and other juvenile disciplinarians may deliberately try to induce this in order to have cause to impose further discipline, it is entirely out of keeping with the dignity of a very serious punishment imposed by an adult.

It should not normally be necessary to secure a girl in position. Most English girls will bear a caning with as much fortitude as they can muster, and while some may cry out, few will leave the position they have been ordered to take up. However, in the case of very immature or spoiled girls, some members of the lower orders and some foreign girls, it may sometimes be necessary to secure them. A girl who has a history of rebelling under discipline should always be secured. By far the best method of securing a girl is to have her held down by one or more other girls. Most girls will enthusiastically undertake this office, and their energetic, sound-hearted English dislike of rebellion together with their good-natured acceptance both of the culprit and her punishment will help to instil in the rebellious girl (often a self-dramatising "victim" or "crusader for justice"), a sense of proportion and of normal values. If another girl is not available one may use a variety of methods including cords, straps or nylon stockings—the latter may seem delicate as they are so easily laddered, but even the sheerest, most gossamer-like modern ones are in fact virtually unbreakable, and, since they are always readily available in female establishments, have long been an excellent traditional standby.

Having positioned the girl one then undertakes the final preparation. The cane was introduced into English schools in the 19th century partly as a healthy progressive measure ensuring modesty (although its use is, in fact, of great antiquity, going back to classical times and beyond). Unlike the birch, it does not require substantial divestment of clothes (although the birch can be and is applied to girls without undue loss of decorum: see page 73). The cane can be very effectively applied over a tight skirt, and usually is in offices and other places of adult employment. Over a loose skirt it is not such a simple matter. If the skirt is reasonably thin, it may be tucked between the girl's upper thighs to keep it flat and taut. A caning may then be effectively administered in many cases. With thicker loose skirts or the pleated school skirt, only the heavier canes are really effective and it is not uncommon for the skirt to be raised. This in itself adds to the punishment another element of apprehension and shame. Having raised the skirt one is faced with the petticoat. This will normally be of a light cotton or nylon and would seem to present little impediment to the cane, however if it is loose it must be tucked firmly between the girl's upper thighs until it lies tightly across thighs and seat. The outline of the knickers and of the tops of the stockings should be visible through the material. If not, it will certainly diminish the stroke. The lightest, wispiest petticoat, if loose, can rob a stroke of its force by "catching" it in advance of its final impact: we speak from experience. This method of caning over the petticoat is probably the most usual, and in some schools and institutions is a compulsory minimum standard of modesty. Elsewhere it is allowable to raise the petticoat also, caning directly on the seat of the knickers and sometimes also the upper thighs. The removal or taking down of knickers is needless, indecent and, in all Government schools and institutions, forbidden. The practice of pulling up the leg apertures of the knickers very high in order to expose a large portion of the seat to the direct attentions of the cane is in our view unnecessary and undignified.

Final preliminaries may include a few "practice" cuts in the air, emitting a frightening swish, and perhaps some preliminary "aim-taking" taps on the seat of the knickers. These are both designed to heighten the sense of dread anticipation and are valuable in getting hand and eye "in" for the administration of the most effective caning. Some mistresses, however, consider it "cleaner" and more accomplished-seeming to go straight into the strokes proper without these exercises.

It is important to understand that a caning is in the nature of a *ritual.* All schoolchildren instinctively understand it as such and surround it with an almost mythic air. Despite the much greater rootedness and cohesion of the modern world as opposed to that of a generation or two ago, we still live in a civilisation that is ritually impoverished, and the ritual of a serious punishment is one of the few that occur naturally in a largely laicised world. Its pain and fear only serve to heighten its intensity and depth and to add richness to the experience (a thing that can be more easily understood now that we have passed the "consumerist" stage of considering mere comfort and animal pleasure as the sole aims of life). The mistress should be aware of this and treat the occasion with both solemnity and "form". Her commands and actions should follow a pattern that have about them a dignified air of inevitability and even of timelessness. The preliminary lecture, the flexing of the cane. The terrible words which signal that the Moment is at hand: "Stand up, Rachael. Step forward. Turn. Bend over the desk." The measured and deliberate raising of the skirt and perhaps the petticoat. The final words of admonition and then, at last, the Rite itself.

The Technique of Caning

HAVING COMPLETED all preliminaries one must proceed to the caning itself. This is a matter on which, as we have suggested earlier, written instruction can be only of limited value. Caning, being a physical skill, can only be properly taught in person. However there are certain remarks that may be made. Ensure that each stroke is a good one. There must be no half-hearted or even three-quarter-hearted strokes in a caning. If you intend to give a lesser punishment, then give four good strokes, not six mediocre ones or four good ones and two mediocre ones. Think of each stroke as if it were the only one you were giving and put your all into it. In particular, having made sure that the first strokes are hard, make sure that the last strokes do not "tail off" in severity. If anything, the last one or two should be given with an extra reserve of force.

Ensure that the cane falls parallel to the seat. It is very easy to strike at an angle, so that the last few inches of the cane are all that make proper contact. This is incorrect. The final length of the cane should be laid "flat" across the whole breadth of the girl's seat. If the cane falls on the upper thighs, there should be an uniform weal right across this broad area of the body (in an older and well-built girl this weal will be over a foot in length, leaving off as one leg curves away and taking up again on the other). It will be slightly redder where the tip has made its impact, but the aim is to make it as even as possible. It should also be as level as possible: the ideal stroke should leave a perfectly horizontal weal rather than one sloping down toward the tip. Some degree of slanting is acceptable, but it should be minimised. Do not, by the bye, be disturbed by these weals. They will pass off in a day or two and are the normal result of a good caning. If they do not appear or vanish very rapidly, then you are not caning effectively.

It is useful to practice caning using a pillow or cushion placed over a desk for a target. The two things you are practising are aim and force. Aim is all important. It is easy for an inexperienced caner to go too high, hitting the hip, or too low, wrapping the cane about the lower thigh. Both are painful, but both are obviously "messy" strokes which lower the mistress in the esteem of her pupil. They also cause unsightly marks in the wrong parts of the anatomy (these are quite temporary, however and not a cause for grave concern). So practise until you can hit the correct part of the cushion accurately and easily. Only then should you begin to increase your force. Do not hold back in caning. It is a rare punishment, and when given must be given properly. If you do not want to hurt a girl too much, then do not cane her.

When practising, remember the old sporting principle of follow-through—that is, do not stop when the cane hits the cushion (or the girl), but imagine the cane passing right through it. That is the only way to learn to give a stroke its full weight and impact. Use the whole of the arm, shoulder, forearm and wrist in your stroke. The practice followed by some senior girls, however, of taking a short "run up" to the stroke is undignified and of doubtful value. Practise and keep practising until you are confident that you can place your strokes exactly where you want them and with your full force. We have heard of prefects drawing a horizontal chalk line across a girl's navy, maroon or bottle green school knickers to give a "mark" to aim at. This is far too undignified for a mistress to consider, but she may well do the same thing with an old dark cushion in the privacy of her study.

Begin with shorter canes: these are much easier to handle than the longer ones—but do not neglect the longer canes. They are excellent implements and no schoolmistress should carry with her the shameful knowledge that she is incapable of using one with confidence. Again, the answer is practice. Longer canes tend to wrap round, leaving livid marks on the sides of a girl's thighs. Like other "messy" strokes, this should be avoided, which can be done by standing further to the side so that the "cherry-bite" of the tip of the cane falls well within the seat of the knickers. Control of a long cane means control of the tip. Practise placing that tip exactly where you want it. Practise daily until you are as confident of doing it correctly as you are of signing your name correctly.

Having achieved this degree of proficiency, "live" practice becomes desirable, and for a trainee schoolmistress or governess this will be easily arranged; for a mother or guardian it is not so easy, but if one enrols for instruction in discipline at a local school or college, they will normally, if convinced of your proficiency, arrange for you to administer a supervised caning either to one of their own pupils who is due to be disciplined or to an outside girl who has been sent for discipline.

*Caning on the Hands**

THE RULE THAT every stroke of the cane must be absolutely full-blooded is sometimes mitigated slightly in the case of a caning on the hands. The present authors would discourage this practice. It is true that a caning on the hands is very hard to bear, but nothing compels a mistress to award it. If she wishes to punish the hands more lightly, let her choose a switch or a strap. With these implements (especially the former) it is permissible to temper the strokes to one's intuitive feeling for the individual punishment. The cane, however, is the cane, and if chosen must have its full value.

The lighter canes are often used on the hands, but a few

* We strongly advise that the reader give her most careful attention to the section "Punishments on the Hand" (p. 80) in her pursuit of this most excellent and highly recommended punitive technique.

strokes from a full school cane upon the palms can often have a very salutary effect. One stroke on each hand is quite a frequent occurrence. Two on each is another standard award. Three on each hand, or six altogether is the maximum we can recommend for a hand-caning, although we are aware that some advanced mistresses occasionally exceed this.

It is important to avoid the mistake that a caning on the hands is somehow a lesser punishment than a true caning. Of course, if one uses the cane lightly it will be so, but as we have said, this should not be done. It is true that lower numbers of strokes are often used on the hands. Nonetheless, stroke for stroke, a hand-caning is (or should be) a true caning, no less, and probably somewhat more, severe than a caning of the more standard type. It should be recognised as such and should not be given without serious cause.

Caning the hands is probably the most difficult form of physical punishment not only from the child's point of view (it may not be the most painful, but it is certainly the hardest to accept), but also from the mistress's. She has a small target which she must hit squarely and forcefully, avoiding deviation of more than an inch either way from the ideal placement across the centre of the palm; and she has a long, flexible instrument to aim with. One should not, therefore, attempt to cane the hands until one is expert in the more usual form of caning. The chalk-line method can be helpful in learning to aim at a precise target, and one may even outline one's own hand in chalk on the cushion.

It is advisable (if such things are available to you) to use a short and not too flexible classroom-type cane when administering your first hand-canings. Only when you are entirely confident with this should you progress to a full-sized and more flexible cane. The ideal school cane for the hands is long, fairly slender and flexible (a very heavy cane should never be used on the hands). This is the hardest to use, but will repay the necessary patience in practice. It whips elegantly across the palm, causing the most intense of sensations, while being quite safe in the matter of lasting after-effects.

Number of Strokes

THE DECISION as to the number of strokes is all-important in the case of a caning. Since there is no variety in the force and type of stroke it is the number alone which determines severity (we are supposing here that a standard cane is used—obviously the type of cane has an important bearing when this is not the case). Having ordained the number, each stroke must be, as far as possible, of unvarying force and severity.

The most standard caning is, of course, six strokes. It is against this "norm" that other canings are measured, numbers under six being considered relatively mild and numbers over, relatively severe. To some extent the use of the lower numbers depends upon quite how rare a punishment the cane is in a particular household or institution. When the cane is used only in extreme circumstances and as a last resort—in a school, say, where a caning is only given a few times in the course of a year—there would seem to be no value in giving less than six on any occasion. When the cane, while still being kept very much in reserve, is used rather more frequently, when a few canings would normally take place in a month or a week, then the sentence of two, three, four or five strokes should be a not infrequent occurrence. The effect of small numbers of strokes should not be underestimated, especially when given, as small numbers often are, on the hands. Sending a boisterous and unladylike group of girls to the house mistress for two on the hands has the most salutary effect. It has the *cachet* of a caning, and the sobering shock-value without being nearly as drastic as putting them down for six. A caning of four strokes is excellent for offences not quite worthy of a standard caning but where their seriousness needs to be firmly impressed. It may also be used when an offence has been committed which would normally merit a standard caning but there are some mitigating circumstances. Again, where, say, three girls have committed a serious offence, but one is clearly the instigator while the other two have merely followed where she led, it may be desirable to give the ringleader six, or even eight, and the other two four apiece.

Four strokes, then, may be considered a sort of second-level caning, with three and five being adjustments upwards or downwards to this. Two (often one on each hand, but sometimes on the seat) is a short, sharp shock. A single stroke is rarely if ever given as a punishment*, though we have known it to be given as a "taste". This may happen when a particularly severe cane is to be used, or when an especially proficient mistress wishes to demonstrate her art. "I am going to give you one stroke, just to shew you what you can expect if this ever occurs again and I am forced to cane you properly." Occasionally a single stroke is given before the imposition which precedes a caning where a particularly severe cane is to be used. This is especially valuable in the case of a hardened or unimpressionable girl who "could not care less" about her impending discipline; but obviously it is only useful if, say, a good Victorian cane is used by an experienced mistress and the girl who was so blasée about a caning suddenly begins to wonder how she shall bear six of those searing strokes at the end of her imposition. Of numbers over six, eight, nine and ten are not uncommon. Eight may be called a severe standard caning. Nine and ten are intensifications of this. Twelve is double the classic number, and represents a maximum in many schools. Twelve well-executed strokes from a standard cane is a very severe punishment indeed.

Beyond this, for extreme cases, one may sometimes hear of fifteen and eighteen strokes, but this is rare. We once heard of an award of twenty-one strokes in a case of stealing in which the victim agreed not to prosecute if the girl was given a sound thrashing. In our view this should be an absolute maximum.

With the smaller canes discussed earlier, numbers have a somewhat different significance. Even with these, the value of two, three and four strokes should not be underestimated. These canes sting significantly, and a small award still has a salutary effect. Six, again, is normal, but the higher numbers may be more freely given. A dozen or eighteen with a light implement is certainly an ordeal, but one which will be forgotten in a few days. Again twenty-one, or perhaps two dozen, represents a normal upper limit, but one less rarely (though still not frequently) attained. If more than this is required, some other form of discipline—a compound punishment, or a caning with a standard or even Disciplinary cane—would normally be considered, though we have occasionally heard of prefects giving thirty—a practice, in our view, not to be encouraged.

* Since writing this it has been brought to our attention that "one on the hand" has become the standard caning in certain schools where the cane is used frequently.

A final point to be considered is the interval between strokes. A caning, being a set number of strokes of uniform severity, is less variable in tone than most punishments, but one aspect which may give it a particular characteristic is this question of interval. Generally, with the more severe canings, longer intervals are allowed between strokes. This lengthens the punishment, allows each stroke to be fully savoured, and underlines the solemnity of the occasion. Where several strokes of a lighter cane are given, all or part of the punishment may proceed more rapidly. This hastens its ending and deprives individual strokes of their full effect, but on the other hand creates a very painful cumulative effect similar to, but more severe than, that of a spanking. In the case of all but the more serious canings (which should always be slow and measured) the mistress has a choice as to the pace of the punishment, and a highly sensitive mistress will develop a feel for this question of "timing" as acute, within its limited sphere, as that of any theatrical artist.

Care of the Cane

CANES ARE NOW generally available, from the ones regularly on sale in general stores for one or two shillings to the carefully graded implements made available by specialist suppliers for anything up to fifteen shillings each. By looking carefully through the selection in your local shop, you may well find a very nice implement at a bargain price. Probably the best course, however, is to go to a school supplier who will sell graded implements of good quality a little dearer than the corner-shop variety but much more cheaply than those advertised in the catalogues. Here you can expect to pay between five shillings and seven-and-six (depending on size and type) for very sound and effective cane which will last for years if properly cared for.

There are two schools of cane-care, namely the oil-school and the water-school. Needless to say, they do not mix. The cane is a very durable implement and a good school cane may last for many years of regular use (a classroom cane, being more frequently employed is usually less long-lived). However, it must receive a minimum of care and attention. Canes tend, especially in warm weather or heated buildings, to dry out. When this happens they become lighter, lose their flexibility and have a tendency to split in use, or even to break in two (one usually loses the last few inches, or the implement snaps off at the handle). This is obviously severely prejudicial to the dignity of so solemn an occasion as a formal school caning. Rattan grows in damp tropical conditions. If you examine the end of a cane you will see that it is full of round holes. Each of these runs the entire length of the cane, and in its natural state is charged with water. The simplest method of maintaining the cane in a healthy, flexible condition is to stand it in a few inches of water for half an hour each week. There is no need to soak the whole cane as is sometimes done—indeed, this can impair the surface—just stand the tip of the cane in water, and it will "drink" it into the long arteries. Some canes come oiled and waxed from the maker's. These should be oiled every month or so with linseed oil and occasionally polished with beeswax. Each of the two approaches has its advocates, and since they may seem to represent a choice between elegance and naturalness one might expect an adherent of the New Sensibility to opt automatically for the oil-school; that is for the elegant rather than the natural. However, the water method has its advantages. It is said to maintain a cane for longer and to give the maximum flexibility. It also makes maintenance rather easier. The weekly "watering" can be put into the hands of a responsible prefect. We make no judgement between the two methods, but whichever is chosen it must be adhered to, and the cane regularly maintained. We should add that a cane may be wax-polished externally and watered internally by the usual method.

Even with the best of maintenance a cane will break eventually. When the end splits it can be taped or even secured with a tiny nail. We cannot recommend either method (indeed the latter could be dangerous), although we understand that the loss of an unique and special cane is an event which one may desire to postpone by such methods as may be available. A point worth remembering is that when a good, but not too heavy, school cane begins to split one can cut a few inches off the end with a very sharp knife—making sure that one cuts wholly above the split portion—and the cane may then be relegated to some lesser use, such as the classroom, where it may give excellent service for several more years. A good slender cane which splits badly or breaks altogether (or splits a second time after being relegated to classroom use) may be cut down to two feet or eighteen inches to make a useful and effective switch (see *The Switch*, page 70).

A Note on
Compound Punishments

WHILST WE have dealt separately with the different types of punishment available to schoolmistresses and others responsible for the discipline of young ladies, we feel it advisable explicitly to draw attention to a fact that has been implicit in many parts of the text of this book: that many institutions and individuals take the view that most punishments of a more-than-casual nature, that is to say, punishments not administered on the spot, but of a serious and premeditated nature ("You will see me after class" or "Report to Miss Jones for punishment" rather than "Take a hundred lines" or "Hold out your hand") should be compound. Even when compound punishments are not such a general rule, there are many occasions when they will be found to be necessary, and they should be a part of every mistress's disciplinary repertoire. Compound punishments are those which comprise two or more parts, usually containing both a corporal and a non-corporal element. These range from such elementary compounds as "You will present two hundred lines tomorrow morning in your fairest hand, at which time you will receive eight strokes of the Senior School strap," to complex compositions for serious disciplinary purposes lasting a week or more and including, perhaps, so many lines per day, various detentions and strappings with a caning on the first and last days. The devising of compound punishments, like many other aspects of discipline is a subtle and complex art, which requires a skilful hand and a sympathetic knowledge of the girl concerned. Those new to discipline should practise devising compound punishments for various hypothetical occasions and types of girl. It is a good practice to keep a book containing such hypothetical punishments, as well as those one has actually given, which may be consulted for inspiration when a compound punishment is needed.

Afterword

UPON READING a medical dictionary one may begin to feel that human life is but a matter of diseases and disorders. Similarly, after the perusal of a work of this type one may come away with a rather one-sided view of modern educational life. Punishment, like medicine, is a necessary part of life, but it is by no means the whole of it. It serves its function when it is required, and we should all be the worse if it did not exist (how much the worse one has but to recall the schools and streets of the late 20th century to determine). Like medicine, punishment is always in the background but much more rarely in the foreground. They are often forgotten, and should be often forgotten; nonetheless a healthy life is dependent upon the one and a disciplined and pleasing life upon the other. This is a truth which goes far beyond the boundaries of school life, for it has been amply demonstrated that a child who is disciplined at school is far less likely to get into serious trouble with the police later in life than one who has been laxly brought up.

Discipline, however, goes far beyond the question of punishment, even though punishment is one of its foundation-stones. School discipline shows itself in such things as immaculate uniform, pleasing address, courteous manners, cleanliness and consideration for others, all of which are so notable in the modern schoolgirl as opposed to her counterpart of a generation or two ago; and this change is notable also in the new generation of young women in our offices and public places—a polite, amiable, well-turned-out and entirely pleasing group of young people for the most part, and a vindication in themselves of the new approach to education.

In order to maintain these high standards, discipline must be upheld in all areas. Uniform in particular must be given attention. The girl who learns to dress and present herself immaculately in school will never—however flighty and fantastical the new fashions she may follow—become the slovenly scarecrow of earlier decades. Not only the outer uniform but such things as underwear regulations covering not only details such as the colour of the knickers but even the precise denier of the stockings help to give a girl a sense of absolute conformity to a standard. For discipline, especially female discipline, is essentially an enclosing thing—it is not an alien rule imposed from without, but a bringing of the self into conformity with her own highest aspirations.

A moment's consideration will show that this is so. What does a girl actually want? Does she want to be beautiful or ugly? Does she want to be charming or repulsive? Does she want to be bright and alive or dull and sluggish? Does she want to be neat or sloppy? Does she want to be intelligent or stupid? Of course she wants to be pretty, bright, neat and intelligent; but of course it requires a certain discipline to make her so. Indeed it was the false and deceptive doctrine of "freedom" cunningly inculcated in the late 20th century by freedom's deadliest foes which was an alien imposition upon our nation's youth. For a generation and more they succeeded in rendering our young people ugly, slovenly, stupid, selfish and unattractive, and somehow managed to persuade them that they wished to be all those things; that they actually preferred ugliness to beauty, ignorance to wisdom, dullness to vitality. This is the doctrine of indiscipline—the doctrine of the slave and the slave-maker. It is the doctrine preached by him who wants a world of passive, mindless, troglodyte "consumers", rather than one of free, intelligent, attractive human beings.

Discipline, then, is truth to oneself, and it can only truly be inculcated by one who loves that self and is dedicated to nurturing it. The discipline of the modern school is the product of love; the free, rich, generous love of the New Sensibility. The love that sees in each individual that which is most beautiful and true, and strives to bring it forth into full and glorious life. It wages war upon the passive and negative tendencies in the self—upon laziness, unruliness and wayward self-indulgence, precisely because these things are least our own; they are the things which stand between us and the lovesome souls we truly are.

It is for this reason that we hold that feminine discipline has a special place; for we believe that this particular love—this seeing into the depths of a being and wishing generously to bring out her truest and most radiant self—is a special gift of womankind, and one of the finest things which the New Lady has to offer the new millennium.

Publisher's Note

In offering the first fully commercial edition of *The Female Disciplinary Manual* to the public, we feel the time has come to do that which has often been asked of us and never yet fulfilled—to explain it.

In its first five impressions, the *Manual* took the enigmatic form of a small but substantial pamphlet in an official-looking pale blue cover, densely packed with small type and bearing the mystifying legend "Ministry of Education Official Pamphlet no. 442/21315/87/A/14".

From the Art-Neo Ministry insignia to the dry bureaucratic tone of its opening paragraph, the imitation was so meticulous and straight-faced that more than one reader at first believed it to be a reprint of a genuine official pamphlet, perhaps from the 1920s or before.

It soon becomes apparent, however, on reading the text, that the "setting" of this document lies not in the past but at some time toward the mid-21st century, at a period when discipline, like culture in general, having languished for a time under the dead hand of late-20th-century plutocratic liberalism, has returned to its own.

A transparent enough literary device, one might suggest. Unusual, certainly; in fact, in this specific form, unique—but hardly so very puzzling.

Yet sensitive readers quickly spotted that there *was* something extremely curious about this book. Its authority was neither bogus nor tongue-in-cheek, but obviously real. The precise and intelligent instructions in disciplinary method did not have the air of phantasies created by hacks or armchair disciplinarians. Even at their severest they remained level-headed, practical and fundamentally compassionate. Not once did they deviate into lascivious excess nor commit any of the thousand and one little practical errors that the mere theorist can never avoid. How rare a thing this is can only be appreciated by those who have some knowledge of the *genre* of disciplinary writing and enough knowledge of actual discipline to enable them to appraise it.

The sensitive reader was edged, by the very *texture* of the book, ever closer to a very remarkable conclusion: that these were real instructions written by people who knew what they were talking about; and furthermore, they were written *as* instructions to others who were expected to follow them and treat them with respect.

The truth about the *Manual* is that it began life as a series of sundry instructional papers on different aspects of discipline. These were not originally conceived as part of a larger work, but were written within an all-female society where discipline was practised. They sprang out of an entire way of life chosen and lived by a group of intelligent, creative women (or "girls" as they almost always refer to each other) who believed—and believe—that the late 20th century has ceased to be a civilised world and that those who wish to continue living in a sane, decent and worthwhile manner must opt out (or, as they say, *secede*) and create their own civilisation.

This civilisation has been known by various names, but by its members is usually simply called the Empire.*

Indeed, the references to *Empire* and *Imperial* throughout the book are intentionally ambiguous. While they appear to refer to a future Government they actually refer to this current "Empire" which does, indeed, situate itself partly in an imaginary future somewhat like the one reflected in the *Manual.*

If anything, the world of the *Manual* differs from the world of the Empire by being rather more "conventional"—for example, where men and boys are occasionally referred to in the *Manual*, if only by way of accounting for their absence, many of the original disciplinary papers assumed an all-female world in which the male sex simply did not exist.†

This new voluntary civilisation, this feminine Empire, has, as far as may be contrived, its own laws and customs, its own authorities, its own life and culture. The authoritative, even bureaucratic, tone of the *Manual*, therefore, is not merely a literary device. There may be no actual Ministry of Education in the Empire and certainly "Official Pamphlet no. 442/21315/87/A/14" was no more than an Imperial in-joke; but discipline certainly took place. The "schools" referred to are not merely imaginary but exist within the Empire, although they may sometimes consist of no more than a weekly meeting of a few girls in a private house. The "children", of course, are the child-selves of the girls themselves (every Imperial girl has several different *personæ* whom she enacts at different times, so that even a group of four or five feels more like a dozen or more—and from the Imperial point of view *is* a dozen or more). Bonded maidservants‡ are disciplined, as are "younger sisters", "cousins" etc. For the Empire is a world which bristles with "adoptive" family relationships.

Occasional papers on such subjects as setting lines, the technique of caning, spanking, birching and so forth, were written *ad hoc* by girls whose experience in these forms of discipline put them in a position to instruct and advise others with less experience. These papers were circulated within the Empire, and often added to or annotated by other hands. Their eminent practicality stems from the fact that they are written by girls practising discipline for other girls also practising discipline. There is no "phantasy" element at all and the reader may be assured that every punishment mentioned in this book has been actually administered and suffered, usually on many occasions and by several different girls..

---

* For a somewhat fanciful fictional depiction of the Empire, see *The Feminine Régime* For a more accurate account of the daily life of the Empire as it is actually lived, see the same Authoress's novel *Children of the Void,* both published by The Wildfire Club, B.M.Elegance, London, W.C.1.

† This man-less world is depicted in various fictional works to be published shortly and also in the magazine *Artemis*. ‡ See *When the Wind is Free: a handbook for the bonded maidservant and her mistress* published by the Wildfire Club.

When the *Manual* was compiled—again, originally as an internal document for the use of disciplinariennes within the Empire—several such papers were combined to make most of the major sections of the book, repetitions were eliminated and differing or conflicting views represented by such devices as "some mistresses hold that…". The official tone of the papers was enhanced, the School setting, already assumed in many of the papers, adopted as the main (but not the only) model for the book and some of the more whimsical and informal punishments (for example a long and fascinating section on pinching punishments, which may perhaps appear some day in another form) discarded as being inappropriate to the formal style and dignity of the *Manual*.

For the *Manual* really *was*—and is—an official book. It is regarded in the Empire as the definitive guide to formal discipline and is regularly used. Copies of the old pale-blue pamphlet are often well-thumbed and the introduction of this cloth bound edition will be more than welcome in many Imperial households. For official use, in schools, offices *&cetera* it is necessary to discard the charming, but somewhat commercial dust-wrapper—even where it has avoided the grotesque "bar code" and pricing in the despised decimal "pea-money". To fail to do so in any establishment recognised by and subject to Her Imperial Majesty's Government would constitute an offence under the Formality of Public Places Act and might result in a caning from the District Governess (though a strapping or a stiff dose of lines for a first offence would be more usual).

A consideration of these last remarks may give the reader an idea of the level on which the "official" nature of the book should be understood. Of course it was not actually published, as it claims, in the 2030s by the Ministry of Education under the auspices of a re-humanised Government and country; but neither are these claims pure fancy or mere literary conceit. They are translations of a reality which exists because its participants have chosen to make it exist. It may be called a game, but then is not every human custom, authority and institution a game? Is not late-20th-century culture (or post-culture) in all its grotesque degeneracy merely a game which a majority of people have been persuaded to play and to take seriously by the power of the mass-media and the moneyed interests which control them? Is the game of pop- or consumer-kultur in any sense "realler" than the game of the Empire, except in the crude sense that it happens at present to be bigger and richer, to control more money, more guns and therefore more people—more (indeed all) television stations and therefore more minds?

This leads on to the other aspect of authenticity so patent in the fabric of the manual. The manner in which it treats the late 20th and early 21st centuries as a bygone period—like the Victorian era in 20th-century eyes, quaint in some respects and horrifying in others, but at all events dead and gone—is too real to be merely a literary device. It could only have been written by people who have spent a considerable portion of their lives *out-*

side the culture of the late 20th century; who are able, even if it is not completely dead for them, to see it in perspective:—not criticising merely this or that aspect from within, while still accepting the whole as "the world" or "reality", but seeing the entire phenomenon from without as the strange and psychotic mass-delusion that it was.

Only those who have long since ceased to participate in television and newspaper culture—and who have created another culture-life of their own in which to situate themselves—can possibly gain this degree of perspective.

Likewise, it is clear that a real and highly worked-out *philosophy* lies behind the book. Behind the enigmatic figures of Mr. Carleton, Maria Weiss, Vemera Lynton *et al.*, so teasingly glimpsed in the text, lie much intellectual activity and many discussions into the wee small hours by some of the most penetrating minds in the world today—one might say the *only* minds in it penetrating enough to have seen through it.

This is not the place for a pen-picture of the Empire, but lest the reader should have in mind a terribly severe and bluestocking sort of world, we should indicate that it is in many ways quite the reverse—a world of music and laughter, elegant dress and romantic charm.

The rarefied æstheticism and refinement of sensibility that animate the book are very much a part of the Empire. The concept of the New Sensibility is far from being fictional, and the close connexion of discipline with this highly-wrought æsthetic spirit is evident throughout the *Manual.*

Discipline also serves to give definition and "hard edges" to a world, which, being self-created by girls somewhat overbalanced on the side of imagination, intellect and the fantastical, could all too easily become phantasmagoric, shifting and indistinct. The stern disciplinarienne as a *persona*, and the ineluctability of her rules, regulations and set tasks, help to create the solid architecture of a world which could otherwise evaporate into a cloud-palace.

The Empire, then, is like a feminine monarchy (or rather a series of feminine monarchies) run on the lines of a strict girls' boarding school (or series of schools) for exceptionally talented and rather bubbly young ladies.

Very much in the *Manual* that seems mere "colour" is reality. The prefects with their juvenescent severities, the reader can perhaps already now picture; but the references to "the first Queen Victoria", implying at least a second—could they be in any sense real? Or the curious footnote on page 103 about the spread of the punishment of "one [stroke of the cane] on the hand" in "certain schools where the cane is used frequently"?

We can confirm to the reader that both correspond to Imperial realities along with much else that might at first seem purely fanciful.

Ladies wishing to make contact with the Empire may write to:
Her Exellency The Imperial Ambassadress, c/o The Wildfire Club,
B. M. Elegance, London W.C.1.